Jessie turned and found herself looking into the muzzle of Snider's revolver...

"Just set right still, Miss Starbuck," Snider said. His voice was as cold as chilled steel, and the long, slanting scar on his cheek was glowing rosy red. "I'd hate to have to kill a pretty woman like you, but I sure as hell will if you try to get away."

Her voice sharp, Jessie said, "Don't be a fool, Snider! Put that gun away!"

"You ain't giving orders here now, *Miss* Starbuck," he replied. "And I ain't got time to waste jawing with you. Now you do what I tell you to, or I'll kill you...."

→►► **WESLEY ELLIS** ◄◄←

LONE STAR

ON THE DEVIL'S TRAIL

A JOVE BOOK

LONE STAR ON THE DEVIL'S TRAIL

A Jove Book/published by arrangement with
the author

PRINTING HISTORY
Jove edition/April 1984

ISBN: 0-515-07436-5

Jove books are published by The Berkley Publishing Group,
200 Madison Avenue, New York, N.Y. 10016. The words
"A JOVE BOOK" and the "J" with sunburst are trademarks
belonging to Jove Publications, Inc.

PRINTED IN THE UNITED STATES OF AMERICA

LONE STAR

ON THE
DEVIL'S TRAIL

Chapter 1

Jessica Starbuck pushed her dinner plate away and slid her coffee cup in front of her. She glanced out the window of the gently swaying railroad car at the arid, sagebrush-dotted landscape, its brown hues being transformed now to shades of gray as night drew closer. The pale green sagebrush and the yellow soil reminded her that she was close to the only place she called home. As happy as she felt to be drawing nearer every minute to the Circle Star, she still wasn't as happy as usual to be returning.

Looking at the sturdy, clean-cut young man sitting across the table from her, Jessie sighed and said, "I'm really going to hate to see this trip end, Harmon."

"Then don't end it," the young man suggested. "My offer still stands, you know. Stay on the train, and I'll show you things in New York that you've never seen before. Be a sport, Jessie! Take me up on it."

Smiling, Jessie shook her head. "You know why I have to get back to Circle Star. I explained that to you before we left San Francisco."

"Yes, I know. Roundup time, cows going to market . . ."

"Cattle," she broke in gently. "There aren't many cows in a market herd, Harmon. Beef on the hoof is what ranchers sell."

"Surely someone could handle that job for you," he said,

1

flicking a hand toward Ki, who sat at one side of the small, square table. "Ki must know all about the ranch business."

"He does," Jessie replied. "But it's my job, when you come right down to it. And it's something I really enjoy doing. I miss the Circle Star when I'm away from it too long."

"Perhaps Mr. Marsden should break his trip east and spend a few days at the ranch," Ki suggested. "It's hard for someone who's never seen ranch life to understand it."

"After hearing Jessie talk about it, I'd like nothing better than to see the Circle Star," Marsden told Ki. "But my business in New York is as important as Jessie's here in Texas."

"I've already invited Harmon to stop for a visit and watch the gathers, Ki," Jessie said. "But he has the same habit I have, he puts business first."

Ki smiled. The expression tended to startle people who did not know him, breaking like the morning sun across his normally impassive Oriental features. "It isn't a bad habit," he said. "I'm sure every language has a saying to the effect that business comes before pleasure." He stood up in a single graceful motion, brushing a lock of his straight black hair away from his forehead. "And while I'm thinking of pleasure," he said, "I must join my card game in the observation car. If you'll excuse me?"

"Of course, Ki," Jessie said, smiling inwardly at Ki's tact in removing himself with such ease, so that Jessie and Marsden could be alone. She watched his slender, muscular figure as he walked with perfect balance down the length of the swaying car and out through the door to the observation car.

"Your man Ki is very perceptive," Harmon Marsden said. "I wish I had someone I could trust as you trust him. You're lucky, Jessie."

"I know that quite well," Jessie agreed. "My life wouldn't be half as easy as it is, if it weren't for him."

"I really am sorry I can't stop, you know," Marsden went

on. "These days we've had together have been the best I've ever known. Isn't there some way I can persuade you—"

Jessie shook her head gently "No, Harmon. But we'll both have two things we can look forward to: the day when you can be my guest at the Circle Star, and your showing me New York the next time I'm in the East."

"I suppose we'll have to settle for that," he said. "When we do meet again, it won't be as strangers, the way it was this time."

Jessie smiled mischievously. "We certainly didn't stay strangers long. And you don't need to tease me again about my being as anxious as you were to get better acquainted that evening."

When Jessie and Ki had reached San Francisco on their way home from their annual visit to the Starbuck plantations in Hawaii, a message from the president of the First California Bank had been waiting for her at the Palace Hotel. The banker's note told her of an offer made by an Eastern industrialist to buy some of the Starbuck properties in Montana, and asked her if a meeting with the prospective buyer could be arranged during her stop.

While Jessie had no intention of selling any of the widespread empire she'd inherited from her father, she felt that simple business courtesy required her to give the prospective buyer a face-to-face refusal. The would-be purchaser had been Harmon Marsden. Like Jessie, he'd inherited a sizable estate, and since he was an ambitious and enthusiastic man, still in his early thirties, he wanted to expand his family's holdings.

Jessie had been attracted to Harmon Marsden from the moment they were introduced. When he took her refusal to discuss the sale of the Montana copper mines with a nod and a smile, and invited her to dinner, she'd accepted at once.

While they sat at dinner in the Cliff House that evening, overlooking the dark Pacific Ocean, Marsden had mentioned quite casually that he was traveling in his family's private

3

railroad coach, and when Jessie expressed an interest in it, he had invited her to inspect it. On the long cab ride to the railroad siding where the car stood, they'd been able to talk in a more personal vein than had been possible in the café. The spark that had been kindled between them was fanned to a bright flame later, while they sat sipping champagne in the car after Jessie had examined its luxurious features.

They'd become lovers that night, and Marsden had arranged to have the routing of his return trip changed to the Southern Pacific's Texas route so that he and Jessie could be together as far as the flagstop station where she'd leave the train for the final ride on horseback to the Circle Star.

Now, as they looked at each other across the table, Harmon took Jessie's hand in his. He said softly, "I hate to think this is the last night we'll have together, Jessie."

"I'm sure you know I feel the same way, Harmon. But I keep reminding myself that it *won't* be the last one."

"It will be for several months, I'm afraid. Unless..." He stopped and looked at Jessie.

"Unless what?" she asked, when he said nothing more after several moments had passed.

"Unless you..." Marsden reached across the table and took Jessie's hand. He went on, "Damn it, Jessie, I'm not good at this sort of thing. I've never said this to any woman before, but I want you to marry me."

Now it was Jessie's turn to stay silent. She was greatly attracted to Marsden, their situations were similar, their tastes much the same. Marsden was not the first man to whom she'd felt strongly drawn, nor was he the first who'd proposed to her, but Jessie's personal code had closed the door to marriage.

Looking across the table at Harmon Marsden as they sat in his private car, Jessie knew what her answer must be. She said, "I can't marry you, Harmon. No matter how I feel about you, I can't even think of marriage now."

Marsden sighed. "I suppose I knew what your answer would be, and I'm sure you have good reasons."

"I have, even if I can't talk about them."

"Then we'll just have to wait, won't we?" he said, managing to smile. "And if this is going to be our last night together for a while, why are we sitting here with a table between us?"

Matching his smile, Jessie said, "I was just asking myself the same question."

She stood up, her hand still in Marsden's grasp. He put an arm around her waist and they walked the few steps to the main stateroom, the largest of the three bedrooms that the luxurious private car afforded. The double bed that took up most of the room had been turned down by the steward, and its white sheets shone invitingly in the light of the acetylene lamp that burned brightly in its wall bracket. Marsden turned the lamp down to its softest possible glow.

"I want the pleasure of looking at you every minute of these last hours we'll have together," he said softly.

Jessie replied by raising her head to let his lips find hers, and they clung together for a moment in a long, deep kiss. His hands moved to the throat of her soft, clinging chiffon blouse, and began to undo the buttons.

Even though Marsden was from the East, while traveling he'd put aside his stiff business shirts with their high starched collars, and was wearing a plain, soft silk shirt. Jessie's fingers matched his; as he unbuttoned her blouse, she undid the buttons of his shirt. In a moment both garments were on the floor, and Jessie and Marsden were standing clasped in a close embrace.

Jessie felt the bulge of Harmon's erection pressing against her, and slid her hand down to fondle it. By now he'd slipped the straps of her camisole off her shoulders and was bending down to nibble with soft lips at the budding nipples of her full, firm breasts.

As Harmon's caresses continued, Jessie began trembling with anticipation. She unbuckled his belt, freed the buttons of his fly, and slid his trousers down his muscular thighs. Harmon continued undressing her. He released the buttons of her skirt and silken knickers and pushed them down her hips, letting them slip to the floor.

Jessie pressed closer to her lover, reveling in the warmth of his soft, smooth skin. The tingling of anticipation that had begun moments earlier now grew into waves of recurring shivers that swept along her nerves, impelled by the gentle rasping of his tongue on the tips of her breasts and the pressure of the firm, heavy cylinder of flesh that was now trapped between their close-pressed bodies.

When Harmon suddenly released her and swept her up to carry her to the bed, Jessie clung to him and did not release him until he lowered her gently to the bed and knelt beside her. She looked up at Harmon's chiseled features as his gleaming brown eyes swept up and down her glowing body.

"Beautiful, beautiful!" Harmon whispered softly.

He gazed at Jessie's oval face, her high cheekbones flushed pink, her generous lips parted to show glistening white teeth, her features framed by a mane of tawny golden hair that was spread over the pillow. His eyes moved down her body, along the contours of her upthrust breasts, and then to the flat abdomen between her curving hips, and still lower where a patch of curls shone between her supple, outstretched thighs and glowed like fine gold in the soft lamplight.

Bending forward, Harmon kissed Jessie's nipples gently and ran his warm, moist tongue around them for a moment before moving his lips in a trail of kisses down her body. She felt the rasping of the stubble that had grown from his smooth cheeks since his morning shave as he puckered his warm lips in delicate kisses along her velvet skin and then quivered with delighted anticipation as he rested his head on her thighs, and his tongue sought her sensitive center, nesting in the midst of her golden fleece.

Jessie lay quietly, reveling in the mounting sensations that began sweeping through her body as it responded to Harmon's soft caresses. She called on the teachings of the wise old geisha, Myobu, to whom her father had given the

6

task of teaching Jessie to share pleasure with a man, and carefully refrained from touching her lover while he continued to caress her. Jessie's body grew taut, the muscles of her abdomen tensed and began quivering. She held herself in tight control until the constantly mounting sensations warned her that the time had come to stop.

"No more right now, Harmon," she said softly, cradling his cheeks between her palms and lifting his head from her thighs.

When Harmon raised his body and rolled away to lie down beside her, Jessie again called on the geisha's teachings as she returned his caresses. Her soft lips traveled slowly across the smooth, almost hairless skin of his chest, her tongue leaving a tiny trail of moisture that caused his skin to pebble when the cool evening air touched it.

Propped on one elbow, her soft hand firm around his jutting shaft, she explored the corded muscles of his abdomen with her tongue, then stroked her cheeks with the tip of his swollen erection before embracing it with her lips. Returning Harmon's caresses in kind was almost as stimulating to Jessie as receiving his attentions had been. The tautness of her body increased as she traced with her tongue the sensitive nerves at the tip of her lover's shaft. She continued until she felt him begin to twitch in her hand. Then she released him and fell back with her head on the pillow.

"Now!" she gasped. "Now, Harmon! Come into me now!"

Harmon responded to Jessie's urgent plea. He moved between her thighs, and Jessie parted them to receive him. His rigid shaft sank into her. She gasped with rapture as he filled her, and thrust her hips up to meet his penetration. Then both Jessie and Harmon were lost in a mounting flood of sensation that lifted them and carried them along in a span that seemed too long to endure and too short to end so soon, until they drew apart and lay side by side, exhausted in fulfillment.

After their pounding hearts had slowed, Harmon said

suddenly, "Change your mind, Jessie, and marry me." He waited, and when Jessie did not reply, he went on, "I'm not asking you to tell me why you said no a while ago, but I know more than ever, now, that you're the one I want to be with from now on."

Jessie waited for a long time before she replied. Her voice soft, she said slowly, "No, Harmon. I'm not the woman you need for a wife. You'll realize that after you've thought about it for a while."

"I *have* thought about it!" he insisted. "Ever since I first saw you, I've been thinking about it!"

"I was afraid you had," Jessie confessed. "I almost turned down your offer to ride back to Texas with you in this car simply because I had the feeling you were going to propose."

"But—"

"No," Jessie broke in. Her brow puckering in a frown, she said, "I can't explain why, Harmon. I'd be a danger to you and your entire family if I became your wife."

"You've got to explain that," he said soberly. "Because I can't understand why you feel that way."

Jessie reached a quick decision. She said soberly, "I'm going to make a strange request, Harmon. I think I owe you an explanation, but I want your word that you'll keep what I say a complete secret."

"If you ask me to, of course I will. But I can't think of any dreadful secret that someone like you could have."

"Let me talk a minute or two," Jessie said. "After I've explained, I think you'll understand why I can't say yes."

Wasting as few words as possible, Jessie related the story of the events that had formed and now ruled her life. She told Harmon how her father, Alex Starbuck, had first encountered the minions of a vast European business cartel when he was still a young man, just beginning to build the Pacific import/export business that would later form the foundation of the wide-ranging Starbuck empire, of which Jessie herself was now the head. She told him how her father had first been invited to join the cartel, and how, when he refused, the cartel had set out to destroy him by

8

any means possible. She told him how they had killed her mother, Sarah, and how Alex had retaliated mercilessly, only to be murdered himself, eventually, by the cartel's hired assassins. Briefly she explained how, after her father's death, she had taken up the battle, aided by Ki, and had continuously fought the cartel's never-ending efforts to crush any and all opposition to their schemes, the ultimate aim of which was nothing less than the domination of the industrial and financial resources of the United States of America.

"You see," Jessie concluded, "my life's really not my own to dispose of. Alex wanted to do so much, but he left so many things undone that even if it weren't for the cartel's attacks, I'd be spending my life trying to carry out his objectives. You need a wife who can look after you, without any other interests to distract her. And that's the kind of wife I could never be."

"I could help you, Jessie. You say this cartel—"

Jessie interrupted him again. "If you tried to help me, you and your family would become another target of the cartel. How would you feel about me if that happened?"

Harmon thought for a moment, then nodded thoughtfully. "I can see what you mean. It wouldn't make life together pleasant for either of us, would it?" Then, after a pause, he asked, "But don't you feel anything at all for me?"

"Of course I do! If I didn't, do you think I'd be here with you now?" Jessie rolled closer to Harmon and kissed him. Their kiss grew in intensity and she felt him beginning to swell again. She said, "Harmon, let's forget you ever mentioned marriage. Let's go on as friends, lovers, with no strings on either of us."

"I wish it weren't that way, but I know you're right," he agreed. "And since we're going to be lovers . . ."

Jessie's hand went to his erection and she said with a smile of anticipation, "Yes. Be my lover now, and tomorrow we'll part for a time, with no regrets, and meet again when and where we can."

· · ·

Tomorrow came too soon to please either Jessie or Harmon. They stayed late in the stateroom, and the day was half gone before they realized it. Jessie had acknowledged that parting was ahead when she put on her green corduroy riding suit, and the sight of Ki moving their luggage into the vestibule seemed to subtract another hour or so from the time they had left.

Even before the train drew to a halt at the flagstop station that served the Circle Star, Jessie and Harmon Marsden had begun to feel distance opening between them. She and Harmon sat side by side, saying little, as the last miles faded away. In the rolling, semidesert country that stretched for hundreds of miles across Southwest Texas from the U.S. side of the Rio Grande, there were no real landmarks for Jessie to point out, though she felt that each tiny feature of the landscape welcomed her home.

As the train's brakes squealed when it slowed for the stop, Jessie leaned forward and peered through the window. She saw the little station and the corrals that extended beyond it. Two horses and a spring-wagon were hitched to the corral fence, and Jessie's heart leaped when she saw one of the animals.

"Oh, look, Harmon!" she exclaimed, unable to keep from sounding happy. 'There's Sun, my palomino!"

"He's a beautiful animal," Marsden said. "I'd like to see you in the saddle."

"You will, when you visit the Circle Star," Jessie promised as she waved to a big, chunky middle-aged man in range gear who stepped out of the little brown-and-cream-painted station. "That's Ed Wright, he's the Circle Star foreman."

Marsden made one more try as the train came to a full stop. He said, "Wright looks like a capable man, Jessie. He's been running the ranch while you were away. Why can't he keep on running it another few weeks while you go on to New York?"

"You have capable people in your New York office,"

Jessie said quietly. "Why don't you have your car cut off the train here and let them keep on running things a week or two longer?"

"Because I—" Harmon began, then stopped short, grinned a bit sheepishly, and went on, "Score one for you. But you're right, of course. Only don't wait too long to come East."

"Just as soon as I can," Jessie promised. "But don't ask me how soon that will be."

She stood up, kissed him quickly, and hurried out of the car to join Ki, who'd already unloaded their luggage on the station platform. Jessie waved as the train pulled out. She was both sad and glad, and she couldn't help wondering how things might have worked out if her decision had been different.

Chapter 2

Jessie had no sooner stepped off the train than Sun began to neigh and prance. She called to the horse to soothe him, but the sound of her voice started the big palomino stallion to rearing with excitement. His ironshod hooves crashed against the corral rails, sending splinters flying from the wood, and his neighing grew louder and higher-pitched when he heard Jessie's voice.

Hurrying to the corral fence where the horse was tethered, Jessie grabbed Sun's reins and pulled his head down, then wrapped her arm around the golden animal's nose. The palomino grew quiet at once. His neighs turned to a softly bubbling nickering, and he stopped his frantic dancing. Patting Sun's massive head, Jessie started talking to him in that special language unique to well-loved horses and the humans with whom they have the greatest affinity. Sun grew quiet except for an occasional whinny.

With a shrill blast from its locomotive whistle, the train began moving. Jessie turned away from Sun and waved to Harmon, who was still sitting at the window where she'd left him. He answered her wave, and she watched the white blur of his face until the end of the train had passed the station and begun to recede in the distance. Then she went back to the platform, where Ki and Ed Wright stood talking.

"It's sure good to see you back, Jessie," Wright said as

he doffed his broad-brimmed Stetson, his leathery features creasing in a broad smile. "The place don't seem the same without you."

"I certainly hope it *is* the same," Jessie replied, returning his smile. "How are the gathers going?"

"Real good, I'd say," Wright answered. "We've finished cutting the hackberry range and the cactus range, and we've got the market herd started on the west home range. The boys are getting started on the South Creek range today, so they oughta have the gather from there drove in by sundown tomorrow."

On the sprawling vastness of the Circle Star, there were a half-dozen different areas where the cattle could find grass during the spring and summer. To keep the herds down to a size that could be handled by two or three men, and to stretch the scarce supply of water provided by the shallow earthen stock tanks that dotted the Circle Star, the grazing areas were divided into roughly defined sections, or ranges. Each had its own name, taken from some distinctive feature of its terrain. In addition to those Ed Wright had mentioned, there were the nursery range, where calves and mother cows were held until they could be separated, and the horse range, where spare mounts were grazed.

"That leaves the ridge range and the East Creek range to be gathered." Jessie frowned. "And they generally take about two or three days each."

"Figure an extra day on the ridge range this year," the foreman told Jessie. "The critters are strung out a mite more'n usual."

"Then we ought to ready to ship the market herd out in two or three weeks," Jessie said thoughtfully.

"Three weeks, I'd say," Ki volunteered. "Maybe even longer than that. From what Ed says, it's been awfully dry since we've been gone, Jessie. We're going to have to split the market herd when we drive it here to the station."

Sam Crane, the Southern Pacific station agent, came to the edge of the platform and hunkered down where the trio

14

stood talking. He said, "Glad to see you back, Miss Jessie. Ki, the same to you. The conductor said you really came home in style, riding in that fancy private car with some dude from the East."

"It was very nice," Jessie said. "But we're both glad to be back."

Wright said, "Me and Sam were talking about shipping the market herd just before your train pulled in, Miss Jessie. He says we don't have to worry about cars."

"Shucks, the SP's got more cattle cars than we rightly know what to do with," Crane volunteered. "Just let me know as far ahead as you can, and I'll have 'em waiting for you."

"How big a herd are we going to have to ship?" Jessie asked the foreman.

Wright said, "Looks like maybe twelve hundred head at bottom, fifteen hundred tops. Sam can't handle all that many with the pens he's got here. I figure to split the herd equal. It'd take as long as to handle a little ragtag herd as it would to drive bigger bunch."

"That's sensible," Jessie agreed. "But you don't know right now how many cars we'll need, of course."

"It's a little too soon to say," Wright replied. "Let's see what we come up with when we're closer to finishing the gathers."

"Like I said, just let me know," Crane told them. "Now I better get back inside and take care of my paperwork."

After the station agent had left, Jessie said, "Well, Ed, you've really kept things moving along. It looks like all we've got to do now is ride home and make those last two gathers before we're ready to ship."

Ki said, "I told Ed that I'll be riding with the men starting tomorrow."

"And I'm real glad to have you along, Ki," Wright said. "Another hand's going to be a big help, especially when we get to cutting on the ridge range and the East Creek range."

"I'll be joining the men too, Ed," Jessie told Wright. "Being on Sun and out on the open range again is the best medicine I've ever found to make me feel good after I've been in cities for a while."

"You know I'll be right pleased to have you, too, Jessie," the foreman said. "You're as good a saddle hand as any man I've ever run into. Now I'll just toss your gear in the wagon and we'll start home."

In spite of her plan to ride with the hands the following day, Jessie had to stay behind. She stayed at the Circle Star's rambling headquarters house, working in the study that had been her father's favorite room, and was hers as well. While she and Ki had been away on their long trip, the paperwork had piled up. Letters, reports, financial statements, and queries almost covered the scarred top of the big polished oak desk. The desk was one of Jessie's links with her dead father, as were the two leather-upholstered lounge chairs and the long sofa.

When Jessie faced a problem that seemed too big for her, she would sit in one of the chairs, which still bore a ghostly hint of the aroma of Alex Starbuck's cherry-flavored pipe tobacco, and lean back and close her eyes. After a while, perhaps a half hour, perhaps only a few minutes, the solution to the problem would form in her mind.

This time the work she faced was routine, but still time-consuming. There were seemingly infinite details for her to deal with. While Alex had made the Circle Star his central headquarters, his reputation for integrity, combined with shrewd business judgment, had resulted in his becoming involved in many other projects during his busy life besides the Oriental import/export business with which he'd begun his career.

During the course of her long day in the office, Jessie went through papers dealing with the problems of the bewildering variety of businesses that formed Starbuck Enterprises. There was the shipping line and bank in San

Francisco, which had grown out of Alex's original interest in the Pacific trade, but the list did not stop there. It had grown to include copper mines in Montana and gold mines in Colorado, a steel mill and foundry in Pennsylvania, brokerage firms in New York and Boston, banks in several financial centers, endless acres of wheatland in several parts of the Midwest, timberlands and lumber mills in the Pacific Northwest and Michigan, interests in several short-haul railroads, and of course a widespread cattle-raising and shipping network.

In addition to enterprises directly connected with the Starbuck holdings, there were letters from politicians in Washington as well as in a number of state capitals, from charities and colleges and from a few individuals seeking help or advice. Many items out of the heap of papers that Jessie faced required only a brief look, but others brought problems she had to resolve, or at least begin to resolve. The day dragged on until the roundup crew rode in soon after sunset and Ki came into the study to find Jessie still at work.

"I thought you might ride out to join us at noon," he said. Then he saw the piles of papers on the desk and added, "But I see now why you didn't."

"It's finished, though, Ki," Jessie sighed. "I can put it all out of my mind and there won't be anything to keep me from getting out tomorrow. Which herd did you gather today?"

"We finished the East Creek range. Even if it's bigger than the ridge range, it's easier to work. Ed decided to get it out of the way because he thinks the ridge range will take two days."

"He's right, of course," Jessie agreed. "It always does when there's a herd of any size on it."

"If you're through in here, I suppose you'll be riding with us tomorrow?"

"Even if I hadn't finished, I'd made up my mind I'd get out of this office tomorrow and let the rest of the paperwork

17

wait," Jessie said. "The ride home from the railroad yesterday didn't even begin to get the kinks out of Sun's legs."

"You'll have a chance to give him a good workout tomorrow," Ki said. "You know what the ridge range is like."

"I certainly do, Ki. All cut up in little gullies and blind canyons where a stray or two can be overlooked. But that doesn't bother me a bit, and the workout will certainly be good for Sun."

"Right now you need something refreshing before supper," Ki said. He went to the lacquered cabinet on the far side of the study, where the teas and tea-making utensils were kept, and opened its double doors. "Water Nymph, or Dragon Mist?"

"Dragon Mist, I think," Jessie replied. "It's just what I need to lift my spirits a bit before supper. Then, early to bed and I'll be ready at daylight to ride out with you when it's time to start for the ridge range."

"We might as well use that bunch over on the downslope there to form the herd on," Wright said, pointing to a scattered bunch of perhaps two dozen steers grazing a quarter-mile from where the group had reined in. "It's about the only halfway level place we're going to find in this part of the range."

Jessie and Ki, Wright, and three of the ranch hands—Possum, Kerr, and Mossy—made up the work party. They'd started from the headquarters in the first gray light of dawn, and the sun was still hanging low in the eastern sky. The foreman had ridden up onto the embankment that surrounded the stock tank, which was low this time of year, in spite of the windmill that pumped its water up from a shallow underground stratum. Wright was sitting with a knee hooked around his saddlehorn, surveying the area. The others relaxed in their saddles, waiting for him to plan the pattern they'd ride to scout the rugged terrain.

"Best thing I can see is for us to do just like we always have," Wright told the group after he'd studied the landscape for a few minutes. "I don't reckon the ridges have changed much since we branded, and all of you know just about where to look. Just ride straight to the line fence and spread out along it, then start back this way and pick up the steers you run into."

"We jes' lookin' for market cattle?" Kerr asked.

"You might as well bring in all of 'em," the foreman said. "I wouldn't imagine you'll find a whole bunch, but let's get the whole herd together for once."

Kerr nodded and said, "I guess that's all we need to know."

"I'll stay close by here," Wright said. "I'll be tallying when you come in, and while you're riding out, I'll cover a mile or so at the edge of the flatland here."

"You got any druthers about which one of us oughta go where, Ed?" Possum asked.

"Not a one," the foreman replied. "I've got the tally we made when we branded, so I'll know when you get back how short we are. If it's not too much, maybe we won't have to come back and make another run tomorrow."

With Ki in the lead and Jessie behind him, the group struck out toward the rising sun. They rode in a group until they reached the end of the relatively level terrain, then strung out in a loose single file when they entered the broken country that lay between them and the line fence that marked the eastern boundary of the Circle Star.

Out of necessity, they moved slowly and without talking a great deal, for the ridge range was the roughest section of the entire ranch. It was a maze of knife-sharp ledges thrusting up at all angles, of gullies and small canyons, some so shallow that a rider's head and shoulders were still visible when his horse meandered along the bottom, a few so deep that even if he stood in his saddle, a horseman's hat would still be invisible to one looking toward the canyon.

There were places where gullies crisscrossed other gullies, and areas of sawtooth ridges that mounted thirty to fifty feet above their surroundings. Level spots were rare, confined to relatively narrow strips between the valleys and the ridges. It was a section of landscape as torn up as any that might be found on earth, a place where someone unfamiliar with the Circle Star and unable to orient himself by the angle of the sun or stars could roam for hours, or even days, without being able to find his way back to level ground.

Weaving through such terrain took time, and the sun was high before the group reached the line fence. They reined in and the three hands looked from Jessie to Ki as though expecting one of them to assign a section to be covered.

Jessie asked, "Does it make any difference how we split up? It's been a long time since I've ridden over this part of the ranch, and I don't remember it as well as some of you might."

"There ain't none of us real downright fond of riding the ridge range, Miss Jessie," Mossy volunteered. "But I've rode to the south of here mostly, so if it don't matter to nobody, I'll mosey on that way and start back."

"I'll follow Mossy and take the slice next to him, then," Kerr said. "Not that it makes all that much difference."

"How about you, Possum?" Ki asked. "If you'd like to cover the middle, Jessie and I will divide up the north range."

"Suits me," Possum replied. "Yell out if you run onto a bunch too big to handle by yourselves."

After leaving Possum, Jessie and Ki rode north in the narrow cleared strip inside the line fence until she said, "If I remember, Ki, this is about where we ought to split up. You go on and start angling back. I'll take the outside strip."

"Whatever you say, Jessie," Ki told her. "I'll see you at the herd, then."

Jessie rode on alone, Sun dancing from sheer high spirits after his long period of idleness. She followed the fenceline for a mile or so, until she judged that she'd put enough distance between her and Ki, then turned away from the fence and began weaving a zigzag course through the cuts

20

and ridges. She set her course by the sun, high in the sky now as noon approached, and let her mount set his own pace and pick his own way except for a twitch of the reins now and then to keep the stallion going in the right direction.

She rode slowly, angling back and forth to cover as much of the badly broken ground as possible. After she'd covered a mile or two as the crow flies, and five or six in the zigzag course dictated by her search as well as by the terrain, Jessie began to feel hungry. So far she'd seen no signs of cattle, not even any fresh dung on the sparsely grassed bottoms of the gullies.

Just ahead on the rocky ledge she'd been following was an outcrop where the ledge widened enough to allow Sun to move around a bit. Jessie reined in and dismounted at the widest spot. She did not tether the palomino, for Sun had been trained to stand when she was out of the saddle.

She dropped the reins to the ground and, after taking a few steps back and forth to stretch her legs, rummaged in her saddlebag. The Circle Star's cook had prepared two sandwiches for each member of the party. Taking hers from the saddlebag, Jessie looked around for a place to sit down while she ate. There was no shade, nothing to sit on except rocks. Leaving Sun where he was standing, Jessie strolled idly along the outcrop, munching one of the sandwiches.

Without the movement of air past her face, as was the case when she was riding, Jessie soon found the sunshine uncomfortably hot. Except for the curling shortgrass that grew scantily on the bottoms of the canyons, there was no foliage on the ridge range, no shade except that cast by a high ledge or a canyon wall. She finished her sandwiches, and with her mouth dry, she turned to start back to Sun to get a sip of water from her canteen.

She had not quite completed her turn when, from the corner of her eye, she saw a flicker of movement on the floor of the canyon below the outcrop. She was not sure what she'd seen moving. It could have been a bird's wing or the slithering of a snake, the tiny, fast-darting body of a prairie dog—almost anything, for she'd only been aware of the motion, and while the fleeting glimpse had been enough to trigger her quick reflexes, she'd not had enough time to identify its cause. Jessie froze, standing motionless, her gaze fixed on the spot where she'd seen the momentary blur.

Whatever she'd glimpsed was hidden now by a triangular spur of stone that broke through the dry soil and protruded several feet from the canyon floor. Patiently, Jessie watched. A minute ticked slowly off, and then another, before her patience was rewarded. The head of a huge prairie wolf, the dread lobo of the Southwestern plains, emerged from behind the rock spur.

Now Jessie understood why she'd seen no cattle in the area through which she'd just ridden. The crossbred Longhorn-Hereford cattle that now made up three-quarters of the Circle Star's herd had inherited range wisdom from the cows which bore them. Almost from birth, they had the uncanny ability to sense the presence of predators and would drift away from any area that their instincts told them was unsafe.

Though she was sure there had at one time been cattle on the section of the ridge range through which she'd just passed, she was equally sure they had moved out at the first hint of the wolf's presence. And, though Jessie had not inherited the instinct that warned the cattle to move out, she was familiar enough with the habits of prairie wolves to know that where there was one full-grown wolf, there was more than likely another, as well as a litter of cubs.

Lobos mated for life, and the cubs that would have been born to a pair in the spring would now be avid for fresh meat. Jessie was positive that somewhere nearby there was another mature wolf and from four to eight cubs. This late in the year, the cubs would be weaned and eating solid food. The food that the full-grown wolves killed for the cubs would be steers from the Circle Star's herd.

Jessie remained motionless, waiting for the wolf to come

22

from behind the rock spur. The small wisps of vagrant breezes that stirred the air at the moment were coming from the west, at right angles both to her and the lobo, so there was little danger of the animal catching her scent. The wolf was nearly a hundred yards distant, and below her, on the floor of the canyon. It was still standing, with only its long, triangular head protruding from behind the rock spur.

Gauging the distance to the rock, Jessie's expert eye told her at once that the wolf's head made a target much too small to try for with her Colt. Even in the hands of such a skilled pistol shot as she was, the long range made a certain shot with a revolver virtually impossible. Jessie wished for her rifle, which was in the saddle scabbard on Sun, more than a hundred paces away from where she stood.

She resisted the temptation to draw the Colt, knowing quite well that the wolf's keen eyes would catch her slightest movement and it would disappear like a gray ghost. Studying the drop to the floor of the canyon from the outcrop where she stood, Jessie was sure that when the wolf moved away from the protection of the rock that now shielded it, she could put at least two slugs from the Colt in its body. She waited for the wolf to move with the same patience the animal itself showed in waiting behind the rock to make sure it could move safely. The contest was now one of patience, of animal instinct against human brains.

Time passed, but Jessie paid no attention to its passing. She kept her eyes on the wolf's head as the animal raised its long muzzle, sampling the scents carried to it by the fitful breeze. At last the wolf was satisfied that it could move safely from behind its protective shield. It edged forward, angling toward the ledge where Jessie was standing.

She waited until the lobo's head was out of sight, the rim of the outcrop hiding her from its eyes, before drawing her Colt. All that Jessie could see of the wolf now was its bushy tail as the beast progressed slowly in her direction. Drawing her Colt, Jessie took a quick step toward the edge of the outcrop. The wolf was almost immediately below

23

her, moving cautiously along the canyon floor.

Jessie took careful aim at the lobo's narrow body, aiming at its shoulders. As her finger tightened on the trigger, she heard an ominous crack behind her. She let off the shot before taking her eyes away from the wolf, but by that time the rim of rock on which she stood was quivering. She saw the lobo leap, but could not keep her eyes on it, for the section of the rock ledge on which she stood was breaking away from the outcrop.

Looking behind her, Jessie saw that a narrow fissure she'd stepped over seconds before was widening. She threw herself backward, trying to reach the solid stone behind the break, but her move came too late for her to save herself. She had no solid footing, and what had begun as a backward leap instantly became an awkward, sprawling fall.

Jessie reacted instinctively. She threw out her arms, trying to regain her balance. The Colt flew out of her hand as the section of rim broke free and she plunged down with it. As she fell, Jessie's head struck the edge of the break in the rim. She was unconscious when she hit the canyon floor.

Chapter 3

When Jessie regained consciousness and looked around, the dust motes that still hung shimmering in the hot sunshine told her she'd been unconscious for only a few seconds. Her head was ringing and she was bruised in several places by her fall, but her mind was crystal-clear and her instincts hard at work.

Her first thought was that her Colt was no longer in her hand. She saw the gun at once, lying on the ground a dozen yards away, and started to get up to retrieve it. A menacing growl sounded behind her from the base of the outcrop, and Jessie instantly let herself go limp and slumped back on the ground.

Raising her head slowly, she looked around. The wolf stood behind her, not more than fifty feet away. Three of its legs were outspread and planted stiffly on the ground, but it was holding up one foreleg. Jessie looked more carefully and saw that drops of blood were falling from the upheld leg, and now she could see the raw red furrow that the slug from her Colt had made when it grazed the wolf's shoulder.

In spite of the wound, the wolf was far from crippled. Its yellow eyes shone in the sunlight as it gazed at Jessie. Its mouth was half open, its black lips curled back in a fierce snarl that showed its long, deadly fangs. It was not one of the small, tan-colored prairie wolves, but a true lobo. Its body was six feet long, not including its bushy tail, and its head almost as big as a human's. Its fur was a dark glossy gray, almost black and its forelegs almost as big as a muscular man's arms.

Again Jessie risked taking her eyes off the wolf long enough to glance quickly at the Colt. The pistol lay far beyond her reach, but she was between it and the lobo. She saw at once that despite the animal's wound, if she started toward the revolver, the wolf would overtake her before she could reach it.

Jessie looked back at the wolf, measuring with her eyes the distance between them. The animal had not moved, but when it saw Jessie turn her head, it loosed another rumbling growl. Jessie froze, but even the slight move she'd made had been enough to stir the wolf up, and it began barking. The barks were not like those made by a dog. They were the wolf's own distinctive cry, a deep, throaty growl broken by a series of high-pitched yappings.

Jessie was not disturbed by the wolf's growls or its high-pitched, staccato yelps until she heard the same cries echoing from somewhere up the canyon. Then she realized that the animal was not expressing anger; it was calling and the new cries she was hearing came from its mate and their cubs.

Only a few moments passed before she had proof that her half-guess had been correct. A second wolf, not quite as big as the first, came trotting down the canyon floor. A quick glance satisfied Jessie that the new arrival was the bitch, and then behind the second wolf came the cubs, six of them. They were only half the size of the mature wolves, but as they came closer Jessie could see that the fangs showing in their gaping jaws were well developed, whiter and smaller than those of the bigger animals, but equally sharp and menacing.

It was apparent to her at once that the wolves were either communicating in some way that she did not understand, or that they followed some primeval instinct in forming around her. The bitch stopped first, close to the spot where

26

Jessie's Colt was lying. The cubs halted when their mother did, but she yapped a series of throaty barks and they moved on past her, stopping between the male and the female, their black noses turning toward Jessie, their yellow eyes as coldly menacing as those of the two mature beasts.

Lying prone as she was, Jessie felt helpless, and in a burst of sudden anger she scrambled to her knees. The cubs inched forward before a short, quick growl from their mother stopped them. Their movement had spread them out, though. They were no longer huddled close together, but spread in a jagged line facing Jessie. She moved one arm slowly, experimentally, but stopped the experiment immediately when the male wolf snarled menacingly.

Jessie did not make the mistake of underrating either their intelligence or their ferocity. Even from where she lay, she could tell that the wound she'd inflicted on the male was minor, and that as soon as the shock had worn off, she could move freely again.

Jessie could not understand why the wolves had not attacked her while she'd lain senseless, but after a moment's thought she decided that after being wounded, the male was now waiting to find out whether she still had the capability of hurting him again from a distance. She could not be sure her deduction was correct, but she was certain the animal would forget its wound and attack at once if she made a move toward her revolver. She was still debating what to do when she heard Sun's high-pitched, worried whinny.

"Sun!" she called, knowing as she raised her voice that she risked triggering a charge by the wolves. "Sun! Come, boy!"

From the ledge above, Jessie heard the grating of the big palomino's hooves. The lobos heard the noise too, and the male growled menacingly. Jessie turned to look longingly at her Colt, only a foot or so away from the forepaws of the bitch, but with even the slight motion of turning her head, both the male and the female growled threateningly. She froze again.

She could hear the noise made by Sun's hooves more

clearly now. The wolves were showing signs of nervousness. The female was growling almost constantly, and the male now put his forepaw on the ground and took a tentative step forward. He stopped at once and rumbled angrily in his throat as he felt pain again in the shoulder Jessie's bullet had grazed. He stopped, but this time did not favor his wounded shoulder, and kept all four of his paws on the ground.

Sun whinnied again. Jessie kept her gaze on the male wolf while she twisted her head slowly, then flicked her eyes upward long enough to see the big palomino's head directly above her. The wolves were no longer watching Jessie so closely. They had seen Sun too, and were staring up at the ledge. Low growls were coming from the mature wolves' throats in a constant rumbled now, and Jessie saw that she had no more time to lose.

"Come, Sun!" she called. "Here!"

Jessie was prepared for the palomino to respond, and the instant Sun began sliding down the steep, almost vertical wall, she dropped to her knees and began picking up stones from the dozens that strewed the ground at her feet. She saw the bitch lobo start toward her, and launched the biggest stone she held at the advancing beast's head. The rock caught the wolf squarely on her tender muzzle, and she shied away.

She heard Sun's hooves scraping the stony earth and glanced around, getting a quick glimpse of the big stallion, forelegs stiff and extended, hindquarters bunched to hold his massive body erect as he neared the end of his precipitous slide. Jessie quickly turned her attention back to the wolves. When the female had shied away after being struck by the stone Jessie threw, she'd moved to the cubs, and they surrounded her now, hampering her movements with their frantic scrambling.

Jessie saw that she'd never have a better chance, and ran for her Colt. The bitch wolf broke away from the cubs when she saw Jessie move, but the few instants that she wasted in getting away from the excited cubs had given Jessie the precious seconds she needed. She dove for the Colt, grabbed it as she rolled over the rough ground, and sent a slug into the female's brain. The cubs stopped by her fallen form and began nuzzling her, their high-pitched yaps becoming worried whines.

Enveloped in a cloud of dust, Sun reached the canyon floor, and the male wolf leaped toward him. The palomino reared back on his hind legs and the lobo's leap carried him into Sun's flailing front hooves. The wolf dropped, snarling, but regained his feet instantly and bore in on the horse, leaping for Sun's throat.

Sun had dropped to all fours, but he reared up again when the wolf launched his attack, and Jessie heard bone crack as the lobo sailed into Sun's ironshod hooves. She was holding the Colt leveled and ready in her hand, but could not fire at the wolf without the risk of hitting Sun. She stood transfixed, ignoring the whining cubs, while the two animals battled.

It was a short and unequal fight, lasting only seconds. Sun was almost as agile as the lobo, and had four or five times its bulk and strength. The wolf's greater agility and mobility were no match for the palomino's flailing hooves. The wolf dropped sprawling, and before he could get on his feet again, Sun's forefeet descended with crushing force.

Jessie heard bones cracking again as the wolf yowled under Sun's repeated blows. Jessie saw that the fight was over. She returned her attention to the cubs. They were still crowding around the dead bitch. Jessie killed three with as many quick shots and scooped fresh shells from her jacket pocket. Reloading quickly, she dropped the remaining trio with well-aimed rounds while they were scampering away along the canyon floor.

She turned back from her executioner's task to see the male lobo lying silent and unmoving in front of Sun. The big palomino stepped over the carcass as though the dead animal did not exist, and walked to Jessie's side, his head swaying slowly, his golden mane rippling along his neck. Jessie clasped her arms around the stallion's muzzle and rested her cheek on his broad forehead.

"Oh, Sun!" she said. Although she knew that Sun did not understand her words, the strong attachment between her and the golden horse led her to believe that Sun would read her meaning by the tone of her voice. She went on, "I hoped you'd come help me, but I didn't expect you to do all the fighting yourself. Thank you, Sun! Thank you for saving me!"

Sun nickered and moved his head gently from side to side in Jessie's arms. He pawed the rocky soil with a fore-foot, and Jessie was sure this was his way of answering.

"Let's see if you got hurt," Jessie said, holstering her Colt.

She checked the palomino's chest and barrel and found no open wounds, just a scored line in his coat on the chest, where one of the lobo's claws had scratched through his golden hair without breaking the skin. When she checked his legs and hooves, she found a swelling beginning in his off-hind leg, and decided it must have gotten bruised when he slid down the canyon wall in response to her call.

"It looks like both of us got out of that pretty lightly," she told the horse. "Now let's get moving again, Sun. We still have a lot of work to do today."

Swinging into the saddle, Jessie toed Sun into motion. The palomino started up the canyon, ignoring the scattered carcasses of the wolves as though they were a normal part of the landscape.

Jessie was the last to reach the stock tank, late in the after-noon. She emerged from the broken terrain of the ridge range and saw that, instead of a little bunch of steers, there was now a herd of more than a hundred head of cattle around the tank. Possum and Kerr were outriding on the far side of the slope, riding slowly back and forth at the edge of the herd to keep the animals from straying, while Mossy was weaving in and out among the steers, looking for cattle that showed signs of illness or injury. Ki and Ed Wright were sitting their horses on the side closest to Jessie.

Ki toed his horse up and came to meet her. He was looking at the empty space around her, and when he got close enough to speak without raising his voice, he swept his hand to indicate the empty space around them and asked, "Didn't you find even a single steer? All the rest of us did."

"So I see. But I found the reason why there weren't any cattle in the area I was covering. Wolves."

Ed Wright rode up just in time to hear Jessie's last words. "Wolves?" he echoed. "A pack, or just a family?"

"Just a family, Ed, but I also found what was left of three steers while I was riding out. That's why there weren't any cattle there. The wolves spooked them away."

"I'll send Strawfoot up tomorrow to see if there's any more around," Ed said. "He's about the best wolfer in the outfit."

"I don't think you'll have to," Jessie told him. "With Sun's help, I killed the whole bunch." Despite the questioning frowns that formed on the faces of both Ki and Wright, Jessie didn't think it was necessary for her to go into details. She went on, "You found enough to make the day worthwhile, I see. How many, Ed?"

Wright's tally string was hanging from his vest pocket. He pulled out the knotted leather thong and ran his fingers down it until he reached a double knot. "Hundred and sixty," he said. "Most of 'em are skinny, but they'll do to keep."

Jessie looked at the sun, hanging midway down the western sky. She said, "We'd better start driving them in, then."

"We were just waiting for you," Ki told her. "If you want to rest a few minutes—"

Jessie shook her head. "No. I had a chance to lie down and rest a few minutes up in one of the canyons. I'm ready to go whenever Ed gives the word."

"We might as well start now, then," Wright said. "That'll get us back nice and early, and since this was the last gather,

31

we can start cutting out the market herd tomorrow."

"How long will that take you, Ed?" Jessie asked.

"Oh, I figure to allow about four or five days to do the cut," Wright answered. "Two days to drive it to the railroad. Does that suit you?"

"It sure does," she told the foreman. Then she said to Ki, "If Ed wants you to help with the cutting, Ki, I'll ride up to the station tomorrow and tell Sam Crane to order the cars. By the time we get the herd there, they should be waiting for us."

"You go ahead with Jessie, Ki," Wright said. "Not that we don't appreciate your help, but the boys and me can handle the cutting without any trouble."

"I'll go with you, then," Ki told Jessie. "Or I can go by myself, if you've still got work to do in the office."

"No, I'm through with that for a while," Jessie said. "And Sun's got a bruise on his leg. I'd like to ride him tomorrow and keep him from getting stiff. We'll go together, Ki, just as we always do."

Jessie smelled trouble the instant she and Ki went through the door of the little office at the Southern Pacific spur, late the next morning. The silence of the room itself was a giveaway, for the telegraph instrument on the high counter that cut the office in half was silent instead of chattering most of the time, as it usually did.

Sam Crane was sitting at his desk, which was littered with telegraph flimsies, waybills, and bills of lading. He looked up, and the expression on his face confirmed what Jessie had already scented before the station agent had said a word.

"Oh, my!" Crane said, a sigh in his voice. "I bet you've come to order up the cattle cars for your market herd, Miss Jessie."

"I told you the other day we'd be coming to do that within a week," Jessie replied. When Crane did not reply, she asked, "What's wrong, Sam?"

32

"I don't guess there's much of an easy way to tell you," the station agent replied. "The trouble is that old Mother Nature got mean and ornery the day after you went on down to the Circle Star. We're in a real bad fix, Miss Jessie."

"Perhaps if you explained what's happened, I'd be able to understand you," Jessie suggested.

"Floods is what happened," Crane replied. "Not just one place, but two. We got bridges washed out on the Pecos and the Nueces both at the same time."

"If that's all that's bothering you, Sam, you can stop worrying," Jessie said. "It won't make all that much difference if we're two or three days getting the herd shipped. Even a week wouldn't matter a great deal."

"That's right," Ki agreed. "Just tell us how late the cars will be getting here, and we'll keep the market herd on the holding range at headquarters and drive it up here when you've got the cars to handle it."

"Ki, I'm afraid this ain't just a matter of a day or two, or even a week or two," Crane confessed. "The wire I got from the division super says both bridges is plumb gone. It's gonna be more like three months or longer before we'll have trains rolling through here again."

"Three months!" Jessie exclaimed.

"That's about the way it is, Miss Jessie," Crane said unhappily. "That was some big ruckus that took place up to the north of here."

"It's funny we didn't know anything about the storm," Ki frowned. "If it was as big as you say, we should've gotten at least a shower out of it."

"Why, that storm didn't even come close to us here, Ki," Crane said. "It swooped down out of the Guadalupes, up above Fort Stockton, and tore across to the southeast as far as Uvalde. Sent a wall of water down the Pecos that was fifteen feet high, and a bigger one down the Nueces."

"That must have been some flood," Ki commented.

"Oh, it was that!" Crane nodded. "Took out the bridge across the Pecos right where that fellow Bean's started the town he calls Langtry, and wiped the Nueces clean, swept away everything along the banks north of Big Creek. The super's wire said we lost the bridge and foundation and a mile or so of track."

"That can be a bad thing for us," Ki told Jessie, his voice sober. "Ed was talking yesterday about what a dry year this has been. One of the things he said was that he'd be glad to see the market herd moving out, because he's going to be hard pressed for water to carry the rest of the cattle until the winter rains begin."

"Yes. I noticed how dry the country is when we were out yesterday," Jessie nodded. She turned back to Crane. "Isn't there some other railroad that your cars can use to get them close enough to the ranch for us to drive our herd to, Sam?"

Crane shook his head. He pointed to the railroad map of the United States that took up most of the back wall. "Look for yourself, Miss Jessie. There's a bunch of little jerkwater lines running out of San Antonio, but not one of 'em runs this way."

"Well, we know the problem now," Ki said calmly. "Suppose we try to think of a solution."

"I been thinking a lot about that, ever since I got that wire from the super," Crane said. "I figured maybe you could drive the steers to the Nueces. You'd have to swim 'em across Big Creek, then cut east and get 'em over the river where the bridge used to be. The rails run right up to the east bank of the river, and I can have cattle cars waiting for you there."

"It wouldn't be the first time that Circle Star cattle have been driven to market," Ki reminded Jessie. "Alex used to drive the market herds all the way to San Antonio every year."

"I remember," Jessie said. "And I remember how glad he was when the railroad came close enough to save the three weeks on the trail, and how much more he could get for steers that had been hauled to market instead of driven."

34

"Yes, I remember that too," Ki agreed. "But driving to the Nueces wouldn't take three weeks, Jessie."

Jessie frowned thoughtfully. She said, "I wonder just how long it *would* take?"

Ki pointed to the big map on the wall. "There's the easiest way to find out."

They went to the map and studied it for a moment. Jessie asked Crane, "Sam, do you have a ruler or something?"

"Sure." The station agent brought them a ruler and stood watching while Jessie measured the distance from the Circle Star to the wavering blue line that represented the Nueces River.

"About sixty miles," she said. "Isn't twelve or fifteen miles about the distance a trail herd can cover in a day?"

"Something like that," Ki nodded.

"Four or five days of driving, then," Jessie said with a frown.

Ki asked Crane, "Sam, are you sure you can have the cattle cars we need for the herd waiting on the east bank of the Nueces, if we decide to make the drive?"

"Sure, I'm sure, Ki," Crane replied instantly.

"Well, Jessie?" Ki asked.

"Oh, I'm not discarding the idea, Ki," she replied. "But I need to think about it. And I wouldn't make up my mind before talking it over with Ed. He and the boys would be doing all the extra work. But if that's the only answer, I've got a pretty good idea that you and I might be starting our first trail drive sometime in the next few days!"

Chapter 4

"I don't think we've got much choice, Jessie," Ed Wright said after Jessie and Ki had explained the problem caused by the railroad bridges being washed out. "That market herd's got to be moved off the holding range inside of two or three weeks. There won't be graze enough to keep it there any longer than that."

"Suppose we didn't ship at all this year, Ed?" Jessie asked the foreman. "Couldn't we just spread the steers from the market herd out over the ranch and forget about taking a herd to market until next fall?"

Wright shook his head. "I don't see how. Dry as it's been this year, we'll be lucky if the grass and water hold out for the cattle we figured to carry over."

Ki asked, "Will we have enough hands to make a drive to the Nueces and still keep things going here at the ranch?"

"Oh, we can manage that, Ki," Wright replied. "This time of year, after the ranches have worked down to their winter range herds and started letting some hands go, there's always saddle tramps stopping by, looking for a job."

"You know the way I feel about hiring saddle tramps, Ed," Jessie said. "Half the time the amount of work they do isn't enough to make up for the trouble they cause."

"If we get in a squeeze for trail hands, I can talk to Will Grant over at the Box B," Wright suggested. "They oughta have a man or two they can lend us for the drive."

"Has Brad Close shipped his herd, then?" Jessie asked.

"I don't rightly know, Jessie," Wright answered. "Will Grant and me ain't particular friends. He's got his way of being foreman, I got mine. But ever since I've been in this part of the country, the Box B has always shipped before we do, so I reckon his steers are already gone."

"I can ride over in the morning and find out if Close can spare us two or three men for a drive," Ki offered. "But I've been thinking about this mess we're in, and it seems to me that if we're going to have to drive as far as the Nueces, we might as well take the herd right on in to San Antonio."

"It'd save what we've been paying the railroad," Wright said thoughtfully. "We'd have the extra hands anyhow, and by the time we got to the Nueces, the herd would've shook down to where it wouldn't be much trouble to keep it moving."

"We've never talked about this before, Ed," Jessie said, "but from what you say, I get the idea you've made a few trail drives at one time or another."

"One or two, when I was a kid, Jessie. Enough to know how to handle as many steers as we'd have in a trail herd."

"I never did ask you how big our herd's going to be this year," Jessie said. "We got so busy trying to decide what to do about getting the steers to market that it slipped my mind."

"We'll ship—" Wright stopped, grinned, and shook his head. "That's habit talking, I guess. We'll have about eleven hundred head to take to market, Jessie."

"That's too many for the men we can spare for the drive to handle, isn't it?" she asked.

Wright nodded. "We'd need two or three more hands. Four is about as many as I can take away from the Circle Star and still have things run smooth while we're gone."

Jessie turned to Ki. "Then you'd better ride over to the Box B in the morning, and see if Brad Close can spare two or three of his hands. And, Ki, what you suggested about trailing the herd to San Antonio makes sense. We'll just drive all the way and save shipping charges."

As things turned out, Ki was spared the ride to the Box B. He and Jessie were still at breakfast when Brad Close arrived. The Box B owner refused a second breakfast, but joined them for coffee, and as soon as the amenities had been taken care of, he went right to the reason for his visit.

"I see you're still holding your market herd, Jessie," Close said. "I'd take that to mean you've already found out about the railroad bridges being washed out."

Jessie nodded. "Ki and I went up yesterday to order cattle cars, and Sam Crane told us what happened."

"Well, you're not alone," Close said unhappily. "I'm in the same boat. Got about a thousand head on my holding range, eating grass I'm going to need to carry the place this winter."

"You're usually the first one to ship, Brad," Ki put in. "What happened to delay you?"

"A lot of little things, Ki. A couple of our old hands got itchy feet and quit, so that put us behind. Oh, Will Grant hired on a pair of saddle tramps to replace them, but we'd have put two extra men on anyhow, for cutting and driving the herd up to the railroad."

"Are you going to trail your herd to the Nueces, Brad?" Jessie asked. "That's what Sam Crane suggested we do."

"I was figuring on it, Jessie. Fact is, I rode over to the river myself, just scouting the land out. I just got back from there last night."

"How does it look?" Ki asked.

"It'd be an easy drive, Ki. No water to speak of in the cricks, but enough for a herd to make do on, if it had to."

Jessie frowned. "From it the way you're talking, though, you're not going to drive your herd to the railroad, Brad."

"I'm not, Jessie. I had two reasons for going to the Nueces. One was to scout the trail, like I said. The other one was to reserve the stock pens I'd need to hold my cattle in San Antonio until I could close a deal with a buyer. Jessie, I hate to tell you this, but the railroad hasn't got any pens, and neither has the stockyards there."

"That's impossible, Brad!" Jessie protested. "Arch Moberly said he was building bigger yards than he'd need for a long time when he moved over to be closer to the railroad two years ago."

"Moberly's dead," Close told Jessie. "He got killed in a fire that destroyed the new stockyards a week ago. There's not going to be anyplace to hold cattle in San Antonio for the next five or six months."

"Surely there's someplace else!" Ki protested.

"You'd think so, Ki, but Moberly owned the yards himself, lock, stock, and barrel. He didn't have any kin or any partners either, so there's nobody to take charge."

"What about the old stockyard?" Jessie asked. "Isn't it still there?"

Close shook his head. "Moberly sold the land it was on when he built the new one. There's houses going up now where the old yards used to be."

"Surely there's enough range land around San Antonio to graze herds on while they're waiting to be shipped," Jessie said.

"Have you been there lately?" Close asked.

"No. It's been two years since I've stopped there for any length of time."

"You wouldn't know the place. Used to be pretty much open land all around it, but it ain't that way anymore. And I hear the people that owns the land that's still open charges an arm and a leg for grazing. About the only place to ship from now is Fort Worth."

"But that's almost three hundred miles farther north," Ki said. "It's almost as far—" He stopped short. "Wait just a minute, I'll be right back."

When he returned a moment later, Ki was carrying a map. He cleared a space on the breakfast table and unrolled

40

it, then bent over it and began measuring, spanning distances between his thumb and forefinger, comparing them with the scale at the bottom of the map. When he'd finished, he looked up at Jessie and Close.

"This doesn't seem to make sense," he told them, "but when you take into account all the little towns a trail herd would have to circle, driving from here to Fort Worth, you'd be driving within about fifty miles of the distance to Dodge City."

"You're right, Ki, it doesn't seem to make sense," Jessie agreed. "Let me take a look at that map."

Now it was Jessie's turn to bend over the map and measure. She took her time, carefully comparing distances with the miles scale at the bottom, and when she'd finished and sat down again, her face was puckered into a thoughtful frown.

"You didn't miss it by much, Ki," she said. "If you look at the zigzag line a herd would have to follow to Fort Worth, and figure on the time lost in river crossings, it would be about as easy to drive straight to Dodge City, if the herd went north between the Nueces and Devil's River. Is that what you're suggesting we do?"

"I'm just saying that it's not the distance a herd would have to cover," Ki replied. "It's the time the cattle would be moving, the speed a herd could make."

"Ki's right," Close agreed. "I did some looking at a map too, before I came over here. I wasn't exactly planning anything except a drive to Fort Worth, but it struck me at the time that a herd could cross Big Creek and move along the Nueces to the headwaters, then cross and follow Devil's River to all the draws that run into the Colorado. There's none of 'em more than a long day's drive apart, and you could shoot pretty much on a straight line up to the Brazos and the Red and the Canadian."

"That country's pretty flat, and it's not completely settled yet," Ki said. "Driving in a straight line over country that's still open and unsettled, and having to ford only two or

41

three rivers, makes more sense to me than zigzagging around towns and farms and fording a dozen or more rivers."

"Ki's got a point there, Jessie," Brad Close agreed.

She nodded thoughtfully. "Yes. I can see that."

"I was talking to some fellows from up in the Panhandle at the Cattlemen's Association meeting last year," Close said. "They told me that Goodnight and Bugbee and Cresswell and a lot of the others with big spreads up around the Red River are still driving to Dodge and shipping their herds east from there."

"I don't suppose there's any reason it can't be done," Jessie said.

"It wouldn't be easy," Ki said. "But if the Circle Star and the Box B divided the cost of the drive, it would certainly cost a lot less than shipping to Fort Worth on the SP."

"Well, Brad?" Jessie asked Close. "Does it sound practical to you?"

"It might not sound practical, Jessie. But it might be the best way of getting our steers to market."

"After what we've talked about, I'm beginning to think so."

"I feel a little bit guilty about talking up the idea the way I've been doing," Close went on. "You know how puny I've been feeling the last year or so. I'm not sure I could last out a long trail drive like the one we're looking at."

"I know what your health's been like, Brad," Jessie said. "I've never been on a long trail ride, though, and I certainly don't intend to miss this chance to see what one's like. And Ki will go too, of course. If you feel like trusting your steers to us, and making the same deal for them that we'll get for the Circle Star herd—"

"Stop right there, Jessie," Close broke in. "You know I'd depend on you a hundred percent. And I'll do the next best thing to going myself. I'll send the Box B cook, and I'll take over Will Grant's job as foreman on my place and send Will too."

"That's fair enough," Jessie said. "Gimpy's a good cook,

42

and I'll take your judgment that Grant's as good a foreman."

"Will hasn't been working for me very long, but he's turned out to be a right good man," Close said. "Well, is there anything else we need to talk about, Jessie, or have we got a deal?"

"As far as I'm concerned, it's settled," Jessie said. "All we have to do now is figure out how long it's going to take us to get ready, and how soon we can get started."

Jessie and Ki reined in when they reached the bank of Big Creek. It was actually more river than creek, its blue-green water rippling between banks of yellow soil broken by huge formations of porous limestone. On the other side of the stream, the Box B herd was strung out for half a mile along the river. The chuckwagon that Brad Close had resurrected from somewhere on his place stood beyond the cattle, and beside it a freshly kindled fire was sending up a trail of smoke into the cloudless sky of the late afternoon.

Jessie leaned forward and patted the neck of her horse, a buckskin pony. "Good boy," she said. "We'll get along all right."

"You're going to miss Sun before this drive's over," Ki told her.

"I miss him already. This fellow and I had a little trouble the first couple of days, but we understand each other a little better now. Anyhow, I couldn't ride Sun on the kind of trip this is going to be. His leg's still sore."

Jessie and Ki had ridden to the river ahead of the herd to the rendezvous where they were to join with the Box B outfit. A roiling dust cloud, still a quarter of a mile distant, marked the progress of the approaching Circle Star herd. Ed Wright rode up and reined in beside Jessie.

"It looks to me like Will Grant's sorta jumped the gun on us, Jessie," he said. "I thought him and me had agreed we'd stop on this side of Big Creek and tally when we crossed."

"I suppose he just got tired of waiting for us," Jessie

43

said. "It doesn't make any difference, does it, Ed?"

"Not really, except I was figuring on tallying the Box B herd when we crossed the creek. It's a lot easier than trying to tally on open range," Wright replied.

"Do you really need to tally Close's herd, Ed?" Ki asked. "It seems to me they'd have done that before starting out."

"Even if they did, I'd like my own tally, Ki," Wright replied. "If I'm going to ramrod this drive, I want to know for myself just how many head's in each herd."

"Maybe Grant tallied when they forded the cattle," Ki suggested. "He'd feel the way you do about it being easier."

"Just the same, he ought to've waited until we got here," Wright said unhappily. "But the Box B herd's across, so let's get ours over there with it. I'll tally both herds at the same time the first good chance I get."

"What do you want Ki and me to do, Ed?" Jessie asked.

"I was just about to tell you," the foreman replied. "I've already got the hands set in their jobs. Booter and Tom will be point men, Strawfoot and Kerr will work the flanks, Mossy's going to be my segundo for right now, and him and Possum will ride drag. I hate to ask you and Ki to eat dust, but if you'll handle the remuda, that'll leave me free so that if something happens and one of the boys needs a hand, I can hop in and help."

"I was wondering when you'd get around to giving us regular jobs," Jessie said. "So far, it seems to me that we've just been along for the ride, doing whatever odd jobs have come up."

"I had to watch the boys and see where they belonged, first," Wright explained. "Trailing's a little bit different from ranch work. We really need more men, Jessie. I'd like to have four more. I'd counted on some saddle tramps stopping by the ranch before we left, but there hasn't been a single one show up since you decided to make the drive."

"We'll probably run into some ahead," Jessie said. "But are you sure we're going to need them, with the Box B hands?"

"Oh, we'll need 'em," Wright said positively. "It's like I just said, trailing's different. We'll be night-herding, you know, and that's going to call for three extra men, maybe four, depending on how big the Box B herd is. And even if we've only got a few rivers to cross, an extra man or two can come in mighty handy when we're trying to haze steers into a swim."

Jessie had been looking at the Box B cattle. She asked Wright, "How many head does it look like to you over there?"

"I was sorta tallying in my mind while I was riding up here. I'd guess a thousand, give or take thirty or so."

"And we've got eleven hundred," Jessie said. "It's a big herd to be trailing, isn't it, Ed?"

"Bigger'n most. But if we can pick up a few more hands, I won't worry too much." Wright looked back at the herd, only a few hundred yards distant now. "I'd better get the point men started on squeezing the leaders together."

"And Ki and I had better go take over the remuda from whoever's been handling it," Jessie said.

Jessie dug her boot toe into the flank of her buckskin pony and reined it sharply around. With Ki following, she led the way around the oncoming cattle and headed for the remuda, which was a quarter of a mile behind the herd. Through the thick cloud of dust raised by the moving herd, they could see Possum. He was riding in narrow zigzags in front of the small herd of some forty horses, holding them far enough behind the steers to avoid, as much as possible, the dust raised by their hooves. When he saw Jessie and Ki, he waved and spurred his horse toward them.

"Ed said you'd be taking over," Possum called when he was within earshot. "I better get on up and give Mossy a hand. Dang steers allus try to pack up when they come to a river!"

Jessie and Ki rode on toward the remuda, and when they were within a few hundred yards of it, Ki pointed to the far side of the tightly knit herd of horses and called to Jessie,

"I'll go on over to the far point, you take the close one. Let's slant them a little bit to get out of the worst of this dust."

Jessie waved agreement and started for her position. The dust was thick in the herd's wake, and she knotted her bandanna around her face, leaving only an eye slit between its top edge and her hatbrim. Ki was already angling out of the dust cloud, and Jessie rode closer and closer to the body of the herd of horses, hazing them slowly in the direction Ki was moving.

With all hoofed animals, tame or wild, horses share the herding instinct. Mankind has used this instinct for uncounted centuries to domesticate and control large numbers of animals much bigger and stronger than himself.

When Ki began to ride at an angle to the direction in which the remuda had been moving, the horses closest to him followed him. Jessie had only to ride close to the leading horses on her side to keep the others moving in the direction Ki took, and in a few minutes they were out of the dust cloud. Now they could see the steers crossing the creek, and Ki reined his horse to a slower walk, holding the remuda back to allow the cattle to cross ahead of the horses.

About a quarter of the herd was either in the water or had already reached the opposite bank. The creek was not deep; the surface lapped at the chests of the crossing steers. Wright was on the far shore, and as the animals came out of the water he hazed them away from the area occupied by the Box B herd. The point men, Booter and Tom, sat their horses in midstream, moving only when one of the steers showed an inclination to separate from the herd and move up or down the streambed.

On the near bank the flankers, Strawfoot and Kerr, did essentially the same job on dry land. At the rear of the herd the two drag men, Mossy and Possum, kept the hindmost steers from spreading out or turning. They were the only two whose job required much riding; one or the other was constantly spurring up to head off a muley that tried

46

to leave the close-packed herd.

For their parts, Jessie and Ki had only to keep the remuda in a compact formation, prevent the horses from scattering, and hold them back until the steers were safely across the stream.

Though none of the men hurried the cattle, they kept the herd moving. It was still full daylight when the last of the steers were safely on the other bank, water dripping from their flanks and bellies as they nosed around, seeking to graze. Ki looked questioningly at Jessie and she nodded. They kicked their horses up, moving toward the spot where the cattle had crossed. Most of the horses in the remuda followed them with little hesitation, though a few in the center held back until the animals around them began drifting after the riders. They plunged into the water after Jessie and Ki, and crossed the stream in a fairly compact group.

Jessie was on the upstream side of the remuda, and she crossed at once, while Ki waited in midstream to haze any of the horses that might drift with the current. Ki did not leave the water until the last of the horses had gained the shore. Jessie saw him start toward the bank, and she turned to follow the horses and hold them away from the cattle.

She saw Ed Wright and Will Grant in the space between the Box B and Circle Star herds. Both men were still mounted, and from their faces and the occasional angry gesture one or the other made, she could see at once that they were arguing. After a quick glance to make sure that Ki was emerging from the water, Jessie toed her pony into motion and walked it to the spot where Wright and Grant were still talking.

She got within earshot just in time to hear Grant say, "Now dammit, Ed, don't try to teach your grandpa how to suck eggs! I'm in charge of the Box B herd, and what I do is my own affair! Brad Close is paying my wages, not Jessie Starbuck! And if you don't like it, we'll just swing down and square off and settle things with our fists!"

Chapter 5

Wright and Grant were so absorbed in their argument that they had not noticed Jessie's approach. They swiveled in their saddles and stared at her in surprise when she spoke.

"That's enough!" Jessie snapped sharply. "Grant, just for your information, Jessie Starbuck *is* paying your wages on this drive, even if the money's coming from the Box B. I don't know what Brad Close told you before you left, but I do know what he told me he was going to say. As far as you and your men are concerned, you'll take orders from me, just as you would from Brad. If he told you anything different, I'd like to hear it."

Grant's tanned face had been growing darker in an angry flush as Jessie continued speaking, but he met her flashing emerald eyes unwaveringly. He had what Texans called a "Tennessee nose," a hawklike beak that jutted sharply from his brow and ran down in a slight curve to a hook flanked by thin flared nostrils, and his eyebrows formed an unbroken line that spanned both eyes and thinned only slightly above his nose. Even when he was smiling, he looked angry.

Reluctantly he said, "Brad told me I was to take my orders from you just like I would from him, Miss Jessie."

"Thanks for being honest about it, Will," Jessie said, softening her voice enough to take the sting out of her earlier harsh words. "Now I've got a pretty good idea what set you two arguing. Ed, did you jump Will about tallying the Box

B herd before we got here?"

Wright knew Jessie too well to equivocate. Without hesitating he said, "I mentioned it to him, Jessie."

"Do you have any reason to think there's anything wrong with his tally?" Jessie asked.

Wright was silent for only a second, then he shook his head. "No. Will knows how to handle a tally about as good as I do. It's just that, well, since I'm going to be responsible for delivering the Box B market herd, I wanted to make my own count. I wasn't finding fault with Will's tally, I just asked him—"

Grant broke in hotly, "You asked me like I was some damn fool tenderfoot that didn't know his tail from a hot rock." He stopped, and the blush that had faded as his anger subsided crept over his face again. He said to Jessie, "I'm sorry I let my tongue flap. It's—well, there's not any ladies on the Box B, and I ain't used to watching every word I say."

"I've heard all the words there are, Will," Jessie said. "But I appreciate your apology. Now let's settle this business about who's in charge, then we'll talk about the tally."

Grant nodded. "That suits me fine."

"Me too," Wright agreed.

Jessie looked from one to the other of the two men and said, "Will, do you have any questions about my acting for Brad?"

Grant shook his head. "No, Miss Jessie. Brad told me just what you said he did. You're my boss on the drive, just like he'd be if he was along."

"All right," Jessie said sternly. "Don't forget it later. And while we're talking, we'd better tie up one more loose end. Ed's the foreman of this drive. Will, you'll be the segundo. If either of you have anything to say, say it now."

Both Wright and Grant were silent. Finally Grant said, "I wasn't trying to push for Ed's job, Miss Jessie. He's got some years on me, and he's trailed a lot more herds than I have."

"We'll get along, Will," Wright said. He turned to Jessie. "Don't worry about us, Jessie. Will and me might not agree on everything, but we've got sense enough to work smooth."

"Good," Jessie said. "Now there's just one thing more. I'd like for the two of you to split up the work among the men so that they all do a fair share of the dirty jobs."

"You mean like riding drag and night-herding and things like that?" Grant asked.

"Yes," Jessie replied. "Ed knows what I'm talking about. I don't want your men to think the Circle Star hands are getting any kind of favors."

"I'll see they don't feel that way, Miss Jessie," Grant promised.

"I'd appreciate it, Will. And I'll back you up all the way when you have to settle a dispute that involves my men." She looked from Grant to Wright and added, "I don't expect you to have any more arguments, but if you do, and can't settle them yourselves, bring them to me. Now do we understand each other?"

"I'd say you made it pretty clear, Miss Jessie," Grant said. He turned to Wright. "Ed, if you think there's anything wrong with my tally, go on and make one yourself."

"I didn't say yours was wrong, Will," Wright said. "What I was trying to get across is that if I've got a job to do, I'll do it myself, and if I want help, I'll ask for it."

Jessie broke in and asked, "What was your tally, Will?"

"I made it out to be nine hundred and sixty-seven head, Miss Jessie. Brad figured we'll lose a few besides what goes into the cookpot, but he said if we deliver nine-fifty at Dodge, we'll do all right."

"You told me you'd counted the Circle Star herd at eleven-twenty, didn't you, Ed?" Jessie asked.

Wright nodded. "That's what my string showed. So we've got just under twenty-one hundred head to handle."

"How many men you got, Ed?" Grant asked. "I didn't count."

"Six, counting me."

"Add Ki and me to the working hands," Jessie said quickly. "We didn't come along just for a ride."

"All I got is four hands and a cook," Grant frowned. Then he added, "Gimpy wanted a swampy, but there wasn't another man to spare off the Box B."

Jessie said thoughtfully, "Yes, we need more men. We'll be driving north along the Nueces, though, so we'll pass that railroad crew working on the new bridge tomorrow or the day after. Maybe we can pick up a man or two there."

"Four or five would be more like it, Jessie," Wright said. "A herd this big's going to string out a long ways. Me and Will are both gonna have our hands full, scouting and riding lead. We need a man or two to spell us some. But that ain't all of it."

"Tell me how many. I'll try to get them," Jessie said.

"Let's see now," Wright frowned. "Not counting me and Will, we got ten hands now. We oughta have four, maybe five flankers on each side with a herd this big, and three night-herders instead of two. I'd like to have three men on drag, if I could. And we could use another hand on the remuda, too. Will's men are going to be putting their horses in with ours when we start off tomorrow."

"All right, Ed," Jessie said. "I'll see if we can hire the men you need from the railroad crew. But don't count too much on getting them, or of anybody we hire off a railroad crew being much use to you. There aren't many cowhands who'll even think about taking on a railroad job."

A harsh clanging of metal against metal rang through the darkness and brought Jessie erect in her bedroll before she was fully awake. The night was moonless, and the starshine did little to dispel the darkness. She blinked and rubbed her eyes, and her surroundings came into focus. The red coals of the cookfire glowed on the ground to one side, and silhouetted against it she could see the short, chubby figure of Gimpy, the Box B cook, beating on a dishpan with a big mixing spoon.

When the clangor of Gimpy's breakfast call died away,

Jessie could hear men's sleepy voices, and as her eyes grew accustomed to the darkness, she saw the hands who'd bedded down near the chuckwagon rolling out of their blankets. The unhappy blatting of disturbed cattle began to fill the air, overriding the stir around the cookfire.

Ki spoke from his own bedroll a few yards away. "I can think of a lot more pleasant ways of being awakened," he said. "At least Ed could have warned us that things would be changing after we put the herds together."

"He probably thought we'd know," Jessie replied, pulling on her boots. "But he had so much on his mind last night that it's hard to blame him for not saying anything."

Gimpy's shout sounded before Ki could reply. "Come git it afore I throw it away!" the cook called. "This wagon's gotta roll out t'the next stop if you waddies expect t' git any supper!"

"That's good advice," Ki said. "If you're ready, we'd better join the breakfast line."

They walked slowly over to the chuckwagon. Neither Ed Wright nor Will Grant were among the men who'd already filled their plates and were hunkered down around the fire. There was little conversation; greetings were confined to nods and forced smiles. Like Jessie and Ki, the few days spent driving the market herds had not been enough to let the cowhands adjust to spending full days rather than a few hours daily in the saddle, and sleeping on the ground in a bedroll rather than indoors in a bunk or bed.

Before Jessie and Ki reached the wagon, the fragrant aroma of coffee drew them first to the big enameled pot that rested on the edge of the coals. They picked up cups from the row that stood handy to the pot, and filled them before going to the back of the wagon. There they found a stack of tin plates sitting beside two huge cast-iron skillets and a Dutch oven, and they helped themselves to fried potatoes, thin-cut fried steaks, hot biscuits, and apple butter. They were starting away from the chuckwagon when Gimpy limped up to them.

"Ed said tell you him and Will's takin' a look at the

herd, Miss Jessie," the cook said. "I been sorta passin' on the word to the hands that they wanta be outa here right after sunup."

"Did Ed say there's something he wants Ki and me to do?" Jessie asked.

"Matter of fact, there is," said the skinny, crooked-legged cook. "He wants you to carry the noon feed fer the hands with the remuda. I got it tucked in a flour sack fer one of you t' tie on your saddlehorn. Just sorta keep an eye on the boys when they dip into it. There's two biscuit-an'-bacon sandwiches apiece, so don't go lettin' any of 'em grab more'n their share."

"We'll take care of it," Jessie said.

"Sack's right inside the wagon, here. You'd be doin' me a favor if you take it now. I gotta roll soon's I can, t' git t' the sundown camp and have supper ready."

"Will you have time to cook supper before we catch up with you?" Jessie asked.

"Oh, sure. I got a mess o' beans soakin' in a bucket in the wagon. 'Twon't take all that long fer 'em t' cook tender. And there's still lots of steaks on that hinderquarter I got tucked in the possum-belly. We'll make out till we pass by someplace where there's a store."

"We'd better go eat our breakfast, then, and let you get ready to go," Jessie said.

"Why, I'm ready right now, Miss Jessie, soon's ever'-body's et an' I get my plates back. I ain't goin' t' wash my pots and skillets before I go, just toss 'em in and take care of 'em whilst my cookin' fire makes coals at the supper stop."

"You know where we're going to stop for the night, then?" Ki asked.

"Oh, sure. I got to know how far t' go so's I kin pull up an' git supper goin'. Ed said t' stop at the fust spring or crick I come to after ten miles, and t' stop anyhow when I make twelve."

"Even if there's no water?" Jessie asked him.

"Well, I got enough t' use fer supper an' breakfast in m'

54

barrel here," Gimpy replied. "And it ain't likely we'll go two days in a row without stoppin' where there's water fer the herd."

"Of course. Well, find a nice place for us to stop tonight, Gimpy." Jessie turned to Ki. "I'll hold your plate while you get the lunch sack out of the wagon, then Gimpy can get on his way."

"I'll do my best t' pick out a good place," the cook said. Then, as Ki started for the wagon, Gimpy's grizzled face became serious and he went on, "I don't mean t' bellyache, Miss Jessie, but it ain't easy fer me, doin' all the work myself. Ed and Will both said they'd git me a swampy, but so far I ain't seen hide nor hair o' one. I was just wonderin'—"

"I'll see that you get one as soon as possible," Jessie promised, not quite sure how she was going to manage to fulfill it. "Just do the best you can until we can find you some help."

"I'll make out all right, Miss Jessie," Gimpy replied. "I won't let nobody go hungry. There's a hunnerd-pound sack o' pinto beans in the wagon, and plenty o' flour fer biscuits."

Ki returned carrying the lunch sack, and he and Jessie found a rock outcrop where they could sit comfortably while they ate. The simple meal was soon finished. They returned the plates and cups to the chuckwagon, waved goodbye as Gimpy drove away, and started back to the remuda.

"Ki, we've absolutely got to get some more hands if we're going to make this drive work," Jessie said.

"There's no question about that," Ki replied. "I didn't realize what a job we were taking on when we decided to drive so many cattle such a distance. I'm a bit sorry I had the idea in the first place."

"Don't be sorry," Jessie told him. "It's a good idea, and I like it. But we do need about four more men to make it work."

"Where are we going to get them?" Ki asked. "I don't have much hope of finding cowhands at that place up ahead where the railroad crew's rebuilding that washed-out bridge."

Jessie walked along in silence for a moment, then said thoughtfully, "From what Brad said the other day, there's a telegraph operator there. Why can't we have him send a message to Frank Caruthers at the SP's freight office in San Antonio? There are bound to be some cowhands looking for work in a town that big, and it shouldn't be too much trouble for him to find a few."

"Sounds like a good idea, Jessie," Ki agreed. "We're good customers, and Caruthers has always been helpful. The SP must be running work trains from San Antonio to the construction job."

Jessie went on, "It'd be worth it to us to pay their fares to the river, and any cowhand worth having can certainly follow our trail and catch up with the herd in a day or two."

"I'll look after the remuda by myself when we get to the washout," Ki volunteered. "You can ford the river and send the telegram. Or, if you'd rather keep your feet dry, I'll cross and send it. If we're lucky, within four or five days we'll have four more hands."

"And a swampy for Gimpy," Jessie added. "It hadn't occurred to me until we were talking to him that a trail-driving crew is like an army—it travels on its stomach."

Confusion was a mild word to describe the scene, Jessie thought as she watched the cowhands working to shape up the herd in the soft pink light of sunrise. She was in front of the remuda, and Ki had gone to the rear of the horse herd to ride drag when they started the animals moving. She was sitting a fresh horse, a pinto mare that she'd ridden only a few times.

Still unaccustomed to their jobs, the night-herders had allowed the cattle to drift during the darkness, and a small-scale roundup was taking place. Jessie watched the men galloping back and forth as they hazed small bunches of stragglers into the body of the herd, trying to merge the Circle Star cattle with those from the Box B.

After so many months when they'd been left virtually undisturbed on the range, the cattle were not used to being worked. They were also confused and tired from their first few days on the trail, and they responded reluctantly to the shouting and waving of the riders trying to get them started. Some of the steers were so reluctant to move that the hand hazing them was forced to ride up to one and fan its rump with his hat, or slap it with a coiled lariat.

Jessie was watching one of the Box B hands—a Mexican whose name was Cujo—trying to set into motion a steer whose dark gray hide was of the shad called grulla. Its color and its unusally long pointed horns showed that in its lineage the animal had a greater-than-usual share of the fierce strain of Andalusian fighting bulls from which such a large percentage of Western cattle were descended.

Cujo galloped at the steer repeatedly, approaching the stubborn animal from every conceivable angle, yelling at it and waving his arms, then his hat, as he attempted to start it toward the herd. The steer paid the cowhand no attention, but stood stolidly in place.

At last Cujo lost his temper. Reining in behind the steer after several unsuccessful efforts, he slid his coiled lariat from the string holding it in place. Grasping the rope in one hand, he galloped full-tilt at the recalcitrant animal, shouting and swinging the still coiled lariat with the obvious intention of thwacking the steer on its rump. The grulla ignored Cujo until the cowhand was within a couple of yards of it, then bunched its hooves and turned cat-quick, dropping its head as it turned.

Jessie's cry of warning came too late to stop Cujo. His horse met the lowered horns at full speed, and neighed shrilly as one of the tips tore into its shoulder. The cowpony reared and Cujo fell from its saddle as the horse danced away from the steer on its hind hooves. The grulla stared down at the recumbent man for a moment, pawing the ground, then started to lower its horns to gore the unhorsed man.

Jessie had seen what might happen when the horse collided with the grulla, and as Cujo was tossed from his saddle, she was already reaching for her Winchester. She knew that range-run cattle would not attack a mounted man, but would consider a man unhorsed as an enemy to be killed. The steer's wickedly pointed horns were within inches of Cujo's chest when she sighted quickly and triggered the rifle.

She aimed for the grulla's head, but the slug missed the steer's skull and shattered one of its horns a few inches above the base. The shock of the bullet's impact twisted the steer's head and stopped the downward thrust that would have pinned Cujo to the ground. The cowhand rolled quickly away from the steer, and while the animal was still waving its head from side to side, he scooped up his lariat before swinging into the saddle.

Cujo's pony limped a bit, but answered quickly to the reins when the cowhand turned it back to the still dazed grulla steer. The steer moved docilely away when Cujo got close to it, and began moving toward the herd. The cowhand watched it for a few moments, then bent forward to examine his mount's chest. He reined the pony around and started toward the remuda.

"He is not hurt bad, the horse, Miss Jessie," Cujo called when Jessie pulled her mount around and started toward him. "A scratch only, but I think better I get another one."

"You're all right, aren't you?" Jessie asked.

"I got no hurt," Cujo replied. "And I don' forget who save me, too. *Su serviador,* Miss Jessie."

"No thanks needed," Jessie said. "Ki and I will keep an eye on the pony."

Cujo nodded and began unsaddling the horse. He made quick work of transferring his saddle to a fresh mount, and with a wave to Jessie, he rode off to rejoin the other hands.

Jessie looked at the herd again. It was moving slowly, a mass of varicolored backs and shining horns showing through the thin film of dust that the steers' hooves were already beginning to raise. The horses in the remuda were stamping nervously. Jessie halloed to Ki, and in a few moments he'd started them following the cattle as they set out on the first day of the long drive that lay ahead.

Chapter 6

After they left Big Creek, Ed Wright moved the trail herd northward along the west bank of the Nueces. Here the river made a huge, sweeping curve as it wound along the base of the Balcones Fault. That massive escarpment formed a natural boundary between the great plateau that formed the central section of Texas. On the plateau the loam lay thick, and the earth was green and fertile and threaded with rivers. It was a land of farms and trees and rolling country that extended to the state's eastern border and south to the Gulf of Mexico.

West of the Balcones, there was not water enough to grow crops on the dusty prairie that lay below the fault line. The great escarpment was the dividing line between the long-settled farmlands of Central and East Texas and the ranches that sprawled over the arid, semidesert plains of its western section. On the lush grassland of the plateau, an acre supported five head of cattle; west of the fault, twenty acres might be required to provide the grass needed in a year by a single steer.

Though Ed Wright and Will Grant wasted no time in trying to get the drive started immediately after breakfast, the job took longer than they had thought it would. Mingling the Box B and Circle Star herds had upset the cattle. About half of the steers in each herd were the new longhorn-

Hereford cross that Alex Starbuck had begun experimenting with before his death. Alex had been led to try crossbreeding by the experiments begun on the big Kleberg ranches in South Texas, but after his murder, Jessie had been too busy to give more than occasional attention to carrying on the work Alex had begun.

As a result, the Circle Star herd was a mixture of the new crossbreeds and the longhorns that had been the basic stock in Texas since its beginning as a cattle-ranching state. Brad Close had shown little confidence in the new mixed breed, and his stock was made up primarily of longhorns, quick on their hooves, as mean as panthers, and as short-tempered as the proverbial Dutch uncle. Even the new cross-breeds retained enough of the longhorn temper to make them recalcitrant at best, unruly when stirred up.

Because of its late start and slow progress, the herd did not reach the railroad construction job until the morning was half gone. The new tracks were still a quarter-mile from the river, and work on the new bridge had not yet been started. Jessie left Ki to handle the remuda, and spurred up to find Ed Wright. He was riding as an extra point man at the front of the herd, pulling ahead now and then to scout the terrain, returning to help the other two point men turn the lead steers when it was necessary.

"I'm going to ford the river here and send a message on the railroad telegraph to Frank Caruthers in San Antonio," she told the foreman. "If we're lucky, he'll send us the four or five new hands you want."

"I don't just *want* 'em, Jessie. I *need* 'em bad," Walters said. "Of course, the herd's green yet, but we can't lose half the morning getting it moved out, the way we did today."

"Well, don't hold your breath, Ed, but there are bound to be a lot of pretty good cowhands in San Antonio looking for work. If Frank finds the men we need today and starts them out on the SP work train to the washout tomorrow, they ought to be catching up with us in the next three or four days."

"It can't be too soon to suit me," Walters said. "I guess Ki can handle the remuda by himself while you're gone?"

"He says he can. I shouldn't be gone more than an hour."

"Fine. And good luck!" Walters said as Jessie turned her horse toward the river.

Gravel and debris from the washout had created a deep pool upstream and a shoal downstream from the spot where the old bridge had stood. Jessie didn't have to get her feet wet; the mustang splashed across the Nueces in water no more than fetlock-deep, and Jessie reined in at the construction shack. She found the foreman and explained her errand.

"I'm sorry, Miss Starbuck," the man said, shaking his head. "We ain't got a telegrapher. The super figured it's such a short ways to the station in Uvalde that there wasn't any use setting up another key out here."

"How far is it to Uvalde?" Jessie asked.

"Less'n a mile." The foreman pointed through the window to a sharp rise a quarter-mile distant, through which the railroad grade had been cut. "That's the trail, right there. Just ride over that hump and you're almost there. You send your wire to Mr. Caruthers from the station."

Jessie remounted and followed the zigzag trail up the hump. Uvalde lay below her, a ten-minute ride. It was a small town, and from the ridge crest it looked like a sepia-toned print. Almost without exception, the business buildings along its main street and most of the houses on the half-dozen cross streets were built from blocks of reddish sandstone, quarried from the cliffs that rose on all sides.

Ignoring the curious stares that the people on the street and the loungers in front of the salons turned on a woman bold enough to ride astride intown, Jessie rode through the sleepy little village to the SP depot. Within ten minutes of her arrival, the telegrapher had Caruthers on the wire in San Antonio. Within another few minutes, the general freight agent had assured her that he'd not only be glad to find the men she needed, but to arrange for them and their horses to be sent on the first work train leaving San Antonio for the construction job.

In a little over an hour after she'd left the herd, Jessie was on her way back to rejoin it. The cattle had moved only a few miles, and even if their hooves had not cut a wide trail that the greenest tenderfoot could follow, the heavy dust cloud that hung in the clear air behind it would have guided her to its position. The cattle had advanced only a few miles from where she'd left them. Jessie caught up quickly and reined in beside Ki, who was riding the flank of the remuda.

Ki had folded a bandanna into a triangle and tied it around his head, with its double fold covering his nose and mouth to filter out the dust that filled the air in the wake of the slow-moving cattle.

She smiled and said, "You look like a bank robber, Ki!"

"I'd advise you to do what I have," he told her. "I didn't realize how much dust a herd this size can raise."

Jessie followed his advice. The dust was already coating her mouth, and she could feel its grains clotting at the corners of her lips.

"I hope you had good luck," Ki went on as they rode side by side in the dust cloud.

"We'll know in three or four days. Caruthers said he'd start looking right away, this afternoon." She looked back along the riverbank. "You certainly haven't made much progress."

"No. It's been slow. The steers keep trying to mill, and then everything stops while the men get things straightened out. You know, Jessie, I'm afraid this might not have been such a good idea. It's going to take a lot longer than I thought."

"We've gone too far to change plans now, Ki. I'll admit it's the devil's own job, getting these steers to move, but Ed seems to think that once they've gotten used to the idea, they'll speed up. I certainly hope he's right!"

Wright did not stop the herd at noon. The pace at which the steers were moving was much slower than he'd planned; he'd set the night stop with the idea in mind that once they'd gotten started, the steers would settle down to the steady pace that would enable them to cover fifteen to twenty miles between sunup and early dusk. The men ate in the saddle, matching their pace to the slow, plodding gait of the cattle. If the dragmen riding in their positions behind the herd ate as much grit and sand as they did biscuits and bacon in the sandwiches prepared by Gimpy, they accepted the dust as simply part of their job.

Even though Ki had slowed down the remuda, holding the horse herd back until almost two miles stretched between them and the herd, he and Jessie gritted their teeth on a good share of hoof-raised sand as they munched their biscuits and bacon. The big grains, grating as they chewed, were not as bad as the finer motes, which coated the exposed areas of their faces and sucked the moisture from their skin while at the same time filling their nostrils in spite of the bandannas. The powdery dust soon lined the membranes of their noses and kept them wheezing and sneezing.

"You ought not to be riding back here, Jessie," Ki said, rubbing his face, trying to remove some of the ingrained dust. "Why don't you tell Ed you want to ride point?"

Jessie shook her head. "I can't do that, Ki. Not after I told him I wanted everybody on the drive to share in the dirty work."

"But you own the herd!" Ki protested. "Or most of it, at least. And I don't think there's a man in the outfit who'd say anything about it if you just rode point all the time."

"They might not say anything, but they'd be thinking about me saving myself a little discomfort just because my name's Starbuck," Jessie replied. "No, Ki. I learned from my father that the way to keep people you hire on your side is to work right along with them when there's a dirty job to be done. I'll take the dust and dirt just like everybody else."

In spite of the herd's slow pace, a half-hour before dark they reached the creek where Gimpy was waiting with the chuckwagon. The little rill where the cook had stopped ran

63

in a deep-cut bed for several hundred yards before it reached the Nueces, and its almost vertical banks formed a natural fence on one side of the area where Wright halted the herd, while the river itself provided a barrier to strays at right angles to the creek. Wright rode back to the remuda while the men were bunching the cattle for the night.

"Couldn't have asked for a better place," he told Jessie, a smile cracking the coating of dust on his leathery face. "We'll only need two men on night-herd, and I'll split the herding job among four of the boys to give everybody else a little extra shut-eye."

"Count me as one of the four, Ed," Ki volunteered. "We've had it easier than the others, back here with the horses."

"No need for you to lose sleep, Ki," the foreman said. "I had my eye on the hands pretty close today, and a few of 'em sorta hung back on their jobs. They're the ones I aim to put on night-herd."

"I still want Ki and me to do our share of jobs like night-herding, though, Ed," Jessie said firmly. "Don't give us any special favors."

"Oh, I don't aim to," Wright replied. "You'll be cussing me along with the rest of the hands before we're finished."

"If Frank Caruthers does what he promised me, we'll have a full crew within the next three or four days," Jessie said. "He didn't seem to think he'd have any trouble sending us more men."

"I'll be right glad to have 'em," Wright said. "Even if the herd'll be easier to handle as soon as the critters get used to trailing, there's places up ahead where we'll need more hands than we've got. I hope those new hands get here before we have to cut northwest from the Nueces to Devil's River."

"We'll set up the picket line before we go up to the chuckwagon, Ed," Jessie told Wright. "You can tell the men you pick for night-herd that their horses will be staked out whenever they want them."

After Wright had ridden back to the herd, Ki untied the short picket stakes from his saddlestrings, and after driving them into the ground, he and Jessie stretched a lariat between them. Jessie remounted and cut four horses out of the remuda for the night-herders to ride, while Ki tethered them to the lariat.

"We'll bring the other stakes from the chuckwagon, and string a corral for the remuda after we eat," she told Ki. "Right now I want to take another look at that map. It'll be too dark to see it if we wait until after supper."

Both Jessie and Wright carried sketched maps of the route they would follow north, maps compiled from the collection in the study at the Circle Star. Between copies of army field maps and charts drawn by surveyors when the boundaries between the United States and Mexico were being established after the 1847 war, they had quite an accurate picture of the area the drive would cross.

"I see what Ed was talking about," Jessie told Ki, tracing the space between the headwaters of the Nueces and the hooklike bend made by the Devil's River to the northwest. "We'll have to cross about thirty-five miles of dry prairie to get to Devil's River. That's a long way for a herd to go without water, Ki."

"We're lucky, though, Jessie," Ki said, straining to see the lines on the map in the gathering dusk. "That stretch and the one just north of it, where the Devil's River headwaters end, are the only long waterless drives we'll have to make."

They studied the map in silence for a moment, each of them trying to visualize what the lines marking the rivers and the string of dots indicating the route of the drive might look like in reality. Neither Jessie nor Ki had ever seen the country north of the point where the Southern Pacific crossed the Nueces River. With the coming of the railroads to the western part of Texas almost a dozen years ago, the long cattle drives had been abandoned in favor of easier and faster shipping by cattle cars.

Even before Alex Starbuck had bought the range land that he'd turned into the Circle Star, the now abandoned Texas Pacific had built trackage to within fifty miles of the Rio Grande, an easy two-day trail drive from the ranch. When the Southern Pacific had beaten out the TP in the heated race to span the southern border of the nation to the Pacific Ocean, and the TP had been closed down, the present shipping station north of the ranch had been one of the first to be established.

Now, looking at the map in the fast-fading daylight, Jessie ticked off the waterways it showed between the Nueces and the shipping point at Dodge City. There were a surprising number of streams for such generally arid country, she thought. Devil's River, the first watering spot after they left the Nueces, was the last of the streams flowing south. On leaving its headwaters, the herd would swing northeast to the Concho. That stretch was the longest waterless one they'd have to cross, the distance even greater than that between the Nueces and Devil's River.

After following the Concho upstream to its source, the herd would then have a short distance to cover to the series of rain-filled folds in the land. These were not true rivers, but long shallow valleys or draws, left when an earthquake rippled the landscape eons ago. In normal years the draws held water through the the summer, though there was always the chance that they might be dry. Mustang Draw, which would be their first water after leaving the Concho, was at the end of a series of three connecting draws, and the water they held would serve the herd until it reached the headwaters of the Colorado.

Above the Colorado were the several forks of the Brazos, none of them a hard drive apart. From the northernmost Brazos fork, it was a comfortable day's trailing to Running Water Draw, and from there a similarly short distance to the Prairie Dog Fork of the Red River. North of the Red, the Canadian's looping coils would see the herd to the Cimarron in a day's drive, and another long day would bring them to the Arkansas, and Dodge City.

Jessie retraced the route to the two waterless gaps, the one between the Nueces and Devil's River and the more northerly space between the Devil's River headwaters and the Concho, and shook her head.

"I don't like these two big gaps where there's no water, Ki," she said. "I don't know much about trail driving, but I can measure miles on a map, and those places are too wide for the cattle to cross in a day."

"Ed's probably got some scheme to get the herd over them," Ki said reassuringly. "Anyhow, we've still got some distance to go before we'll have to worry about them. Let's go eat supper, Jessie. Those biscuit-and-bacon sandwiches we had at noon didn't exactly make what I'd call a meal."

During the next four days the herd moved steadily north. Late in the afternoon of the third day, the arrival of the new men sent by the SP agent from San Antonio relieved the strain on the Box B and Circle Star men, who could now get three nights of uninterrupted sleep instead of only two in the rotation of riding night-herd. The new hands—Rader, Hedley, Meyers, and Slaton—put an extra strain on Gimpy, but the fifth arrival—a diminutive youth called, predictably, Peewee—was assigned to the cook as a swampy, which took the edge off Gimpy's complaints of being overworked.

By the time they reached the headwaters of the Nueces, the routines of the drive had become established. Shortly after midnight, one of the night-herders would rouse Gimpy, and the cook would prepare breakfast and a flour sack full of sandwiches for the hand's lunch. As soon as the crew had finished eating, Gimpy and his new swampy took off for the next night stop, which had been chosen by Ed Wright, who scouted the route in advance each afternoon. Jessie and Ki would have hurried through their breakfasts and returned to the remuda to choose the horses the men would ride for half the day. In less than an hour after being roused, the herd would be set into motion.

Each day, things seemed to go a bit more smoothly. The crew had become accustomed to sleeping on the ground instead of on a mattress in a bunkhouse, and to being roused before daylight by Gimpy beating on the bottom of a skillet. They'd learned to eat more heartily at breakfast and supper to compensate for a scanty midday meal of biscuits and ham or bacon munched in the saddle, and to doze in the saddle while the herd plodded ahead to make up for the sleep lost when riding night-herd.

Just as the men adapted to change, so did the cattle. They lost the feistiness they'd brought with them from their static life on the range, where they might move only a mile or two a day while grazing, and settled down to grazing at night after a long day of almost constant movement. On the afternoon when they arrived at the little weblike cluster of spring-fed creeks that formed the headwaters of the Nueces, Ed Wright rode through the herd in the fading daylight. He wove in and out among the grazing cattle, checking their condition, and expressed his satisfaction.

"We're in a lot better shape than I'd figured to be," the foreman told Jessie as he hunkered down beside her and Ki with his supper plate. "We'll hold the herd here all day tomorrow, and give the critters a chance to drink up and fill their bellies good. When I scouted today, I didn't see a single draw that had any water in it. It's going to be a dry drive all the way to Devil's River."

"Can the herd make it in a day?" Jessie asked.

"Not likely. But the moon's full now, so I figure to get a real early start and move as fast as the men can roust the herd. If we're lucky, we'll get across the bad stretch by midnight."

Chapter 7

Until the sun came up and the breeze began to fail, the morning had been cool and pleasant. There was the usual amount of fine dust hanging in a cloud over the herd and behind it, but Jessie and Ki could avoid much of the dust by hazing the remuda to one side. As the sun rose higher, the breeze lost its pleasant softness. It blew warm for an hour or so; then, when it stirred at all, its touch was hot.

Soon after they left the river, the land became desolate. There were no trees and little other vegetation. Mesquite grew in low-spreading clumps; clusters of prickly pear rose abruptly from the bare ground in waist-high patches of olive green; here and there a yucca stalk reared head-tall from the ball of yellow streamers that had been its leaves. An occasional cholla lizard scampered across the bare soil; the lizards' bodies were the same color as the soil, and the little scurrying creatures were almost invisible, their movements marked only by the black shadow their long oval bodies cast on the ground below them.

By noon the sunshine's glare, reflected from the light yellowish soil, was stabbing into the eyes of the trail crew in spite of their broad-brimmed hats. When the day aged and the sun slid down the bright, cloudless western sky, its rays began to sting and then to burn. The heat was not great, but it was constant.

Sweat that had been a light film of moisture grew into drops that rolled down cheeks and dripped off noses. The sweat soon soaked the bandannas which by now all the riders had tied around the lower part of their faces. The dust clung to the wet cloth of the gaudy kerchiefs, and though at the day's start they might have been red or blue, all of them had become a uniform tan.

During the last few hours of the dying day, the sun stabbed into the riders' eyes, its reddening rays as sharp as needles. The cattle began to blat even before daylight faded. They had gotten accustomed to stopping before sunset, and being allowed to graze and drink. Some of the steers in the rear began to drop back. The herd's shape changed slowly. Instead of being a rough square, it became a long oval.

A few of the reluctant steers did nothing more than slow their pace, but occasionally one of the animals would stop and stand, swaying gently, its thick-lashed eyes half closed. The men riding drag were kept busy; they rode twice as far as the point men and flankers, zigzagging back and forth behind the slowly moving cattle, hazing the laggards ahead to keep them with the main body.

With only forty-odd horses to look after, Jessie and Ki had a relatively easy job. The horses were not as ornery as the steers. Only about a third of them were corral-horses, trained to cut a single steer out of a herd and to respond to the pressure of its rider's knee or toe. Most of them were newly broken broncos, spares from the horse pastures of the Box B or the Circle Star, surplus animals that would be sold when the steers were disposed of, but except for two or three walleyed mustangs, they traveled more docilely than did the steers. All that Jessie and Ki needed to do to keep the remuda in a compact group was to circle the animals each hour or so and look back occasionally to make sure none of them had cut away from the herd.

"I wonder if Ed's going to stop and rest the herd for a while before dark," Jessie said to Ki as they met and reined up to ride side by side for a few moments during one of their periodic circuits.

"I wouldn't, in his place," Ki replied. "It's getting too late for that now. If the herd stops, it's likely to scatter, and the boys would have a tough time getting it moving again."

"There's always that to think of, I guess," Jessie agreed. "And even with a full moon, it'd be almost impossible to form up the herd in the dark without losing a few head."

Before the last rays of sunset died away, the nearly full moon that had been hanging like a pale ghost in the sky since late in the afternoon began to glow. The day ended without the usual long period of twilight, and the night was not really dark. Still, the cattle grew restless after the sun left the sky. The herd slowed down perceptibly, but Ed Wright did not call a halt, even when their advance became a snail's slow crawl over a landscape that was now bathed in silver.

"We'll tough it out," Wright told Jessie when he came to change to a fresh horse, the third he'd ridden that day. "We've got the night's back broke now. And when we hit the river, we'll loose-herd and let the critters rest all day. I made sure when I scouted that there's enough graze to hold the herd that long."

"You're the trail boss," Jessie said. "But I'll bet I'm not the only one in the outfit who'd stop right now if somebody offered me a sandwich and a cup of coffee."

Wright swung his saddle over to the fresh horse before he replied, "You're not the only one in the outfit who's told me that in the last couple of hours, Jessie. I got to admit I made a mistake, not telling Gimpy to fix a bunch of extra sandwiches."

"I never saw a cowhand yet who was really happy," Ki put in. "Even if you'd remembered, they'd have griped because they didn't get hot coffee too."

"How are your new men working out, Ed?" Jessie asked. "I've wanted to watch them, but being back here with the remuda, the only time I've seen them is when they come back for a fresh horse or when we're eating."

"I've tried to keep an eye on them, Jessie, but it's not

easy when you're hopping around the way I've been doing," the foreman replied. "There's only one of them who don't seem to fit in with the other hands—that's Rader. He acts sorta stand-offish. Hedley and Slaton and Meyers, they're right at home. And Gimpy's not bellyachin' so much, now that he's got Peewee."

"That's good," Jessie said. "And I've noticed that you and Will Grant seem to have worked out any differences you might have had when we started."

"Oh, Will's all right, Jessie. I guess I'd have got riled if I'd been in his boots the other day." Wright finished testing the saddle cinch and settled his hat level on his head again. "Well, I got to be gettin' on. Seems like the boys feel better about things if they catch sight of me once in a while."

"How much longer before we get to Devil's River?" Ki asked as the foreman swung into the saddle.

"Another hour, not more'n two. When I ride the herd this next time, I'll tell the boys to chouse 'em a little and move faster. It's coming on for moonset, and I want the critters there and settled down while we can still see what we're doing."

A pinpoint of light, too low and too orange-hued to be a star, guided them to the place Wright had chosen for their stop. Soon after Wright and the point riders saw the light of Gimpy's cookfire, the cattle smelled the water. The lead steers began blatting and moving at a quicker pace.

Shouts and the sharp staccato of the ponies' shod hooves soon rose above the lowing and the more subdued thudding of steer hooves as the flankers began wheeling at a gallop along the sides of the herd, hazing back into the mass of undulating backs and shining horns the steers that tried to break away and hurry to the river. The men worked at a disadvantage in the dark, for they could not see the traditional hand signals used by trail bosses, which Wright gave them in daylight to guide their moves.

Though the full crew was riding, the restlessness of the impatient cattle kept not only the flankers and drag men in constant motion, but forced the point men to drop back now and then when bulges threatened to break the herd. Toward the rear of the hurrying cattle, the dust rose in a thicker cloud, forcing the drag men to stay closer than usual to the steers.

Jessie and Ki could see little in the waning moonlight. They were kept busy as the excitement of the steers infected the horses, and the remuda began to lose its usually compact formation. The horses gradually spread into a crescent, and Jessie spurred across the front of the animals until she reached Ki, who was trying without much success to haze the ponies at the tip of the arc back toward its center.

Jessie pulled her bandanna down and called, "We're going to need some help! I'll get one of the drag men to drop back and help us hold the horses and tighten them up before they get out of hand!"

At Ki's nod, she wheeled her mustang and galloped toward the rear of the herd. The dust was thickest just behind the hurrying steers, and she angled along in zigzags, peering through the haze as she tried to avoid stragglers. She saw one of the drag men just ahead and reined in when she was close enough to make herself heard above the chorus of blatting that mingled with the muted thunder of the cattle hooves.

"We need help to bunch up the remuda!" she called. "Come ride guide while Ki and I haze the points together!"

His voice muffled through the bandanna that covered his mouth, the man replied, "Wright told me to stay with the drag!"

Jessie could see the man only dimly, but she was sure any of the Circle Star hands would have responded without hesitation, and she placed him as one of the Box B men or one of the trio from San Antonio that had just joined the drive.

"Never mind what Ed told you!" she said. "If he says

anything to you, tell him I'm responsible for taking you off your position!"

After a moment's hesitation, the rider nodded. Jessie yanked the reins of her pony around and started back toward the remuda. She turned once to be sure the hand was following her, and saw him a few yards behind her. Darkness and dust still hid the remuda from her. Judging her position by the muted tattoo of the hooves of the horse herd ahead, Jessie reined in.

Turning, she saw the drag man a short distance behind her. She motioned for him to ride closer and saw his horse leap ahead. The distance between them was not great. When the man did not rein in as he came closer, Jessie frowned and waved for him to come alongside. Instead, he came charging directly at her.

Jessie yanked the reins of her pony, but before the animal could move, the other rider crashed into her mount. He brought up his arm, reaching for Jessie, as their horses collided. Jessie could not ward off the outthrust hand that caught her shoulder and sent her toppling from the saddle. She had barely enough time to kick her feet free of the stirrups to prevent the horse from dragging her when the impact threw her to the ground. Fortunately, Ki had long ago taught her the art of falling correctly, the first and one of the most important aspects of his own martial-arts training.

As she fell backwards from the horse, Jessie tucked her head forward and curled her back to roll with the impact. The landing was still a bit jarring, but nothing to what it would have been if she'd landed flat on her back. Extending one arm, she slapped the ground to further absorb the shock, and simply continued her backward roll, coming all the way over until, within a second, she was on her feet, unhurt. She could see the remuda now through the darkness and haze, only a few yards away. The ironshod hooves of the horses were loud in her ears as they rushed toward her. She grabbed for the saddlehorn of her pony, missed it, but managed to get a precarious hold on the cantle. Using the leverage of her forearms, she leaped onto the pony's back before it danced away.

She landed on the horse's rump instead of in the saddle. Her feet could not reach the stirrups, but she leaned forward quickly and grabbed the saddlehorn. The pony reared, but she held herself in place while the horses of the remuda swept up around them, the excited mustangs bumping her horse as their rush carried Jessie and her mount with them.

Clinging to the saddlehorn with one hand, Jessie waited until the clot of horses around her parted and her own pony was moving along with the others, then she pulled herself forward into the saddle and got her feet in the stirrups. After several misses, she got hold of the reins and began pulling up the horse. Safe at last, she could look around for the first time. The rider who'd tried to kill her had vanished, lost in the gloom.

Jessie did not waste time trying to follow the man. There was work to be done that would not wait. Her hands adept on the reins, she worked her mount out of the horse herd and circled the rushing animals until she'd found Ki. He'd seen the futility of trying to hold back the remuda's headlong rush, and was on the herd's flank, trying to keep the beasts from scattering. Jessie rode alongside him.

"Whatever's to be done, we'll have to do ourselves," she said, raising her voice above the thudding of the horses' hooves.

"I don't think we need to do much of anything," Ki replied, pointing ahead.

Jessie looked, and saw the figures of Gimpy and his young swampy silhouetted against the cookfire, now less than a half-mile distant. Beyond the fire she could make out the white canvas top of the chuckwagon on the far side of the blaze. In front of the herd and along its flank she could see the hands galloping back and forth, turning the cattle away from the fire.

"You're right," she agreed. "The best thing we can do

now is to keep the horses bunched as much as possible. They'll smell the water pretty soon, and head for the river. We can set the stakes for the rope corral while they're drinking, and haze them into it without any trouble."

Ki nodded and said, "Ed's getting the cattle turned toward the river now. The horses will follow them. If you'll keep an eye on them, I'll ride ahead and get the stakes and ropes."

Jessie nodded and watched Ki's back until it disappeared in the darkness. The moon was just beginning to dip below the horizon, no longer silver now, but a dull gray disk seen through the dust-haze. Jessie began riding in a figure-eight beside the horses as they turned with the cattle, making an occasional sweep in front of them to keep the horses from mingling with the steers.

Slowly the herd began moving to her left, the cattle starting to string out as they reached the water. Within a few more minutes she could glimpse an occasional flash of silver from the surface of Devil's River. The horses were smelling the water now, and she did not try to stop them when they moved in the direction the cattle had taken. She spurred up to place herself between the remuda and the herd, and by the time Ki returned with the stakes and ropes for the corral, the horses had settled down to drink.

While they set the corkscrew-pointed stakes in the hard-baked soil, and strung the ropes in the loop-eyes of the stakes to form a temporary corral, Jessie told Ki of her narrow escape.

"And you couldn't identify the man?" he asked when she'd finished.

"No. Between the darkness and the dust, I never did get a good look at him. And it didn't occur to me to ask his name when I first ran into him."

"Would you know him again if you saw him?"

"I'm not sure I would, Ki." Jessie frowned. "He had on a light-colored Stetson, but I'm not sure whether it was white or gray or tan."

"That doesn't help us much, does it? A lot of our own

76

men and some of the hands from the Box B wear light-colored hats."

"They all dress pretty much the same, too," Jessie agreed. "And I couldn't tell one color of shirt or jeans from another, in the dark."

"You know what I'm thinking," Ki said.

"Yes. It smells like the cartel to me, too. But that does narrow it down, Ki. He has to be one of the men Frank Caruthers sent us from San Antonio."

"That's the answer, of course," Ki nodded. "We've been pretty sure ever since that brush we had at Outlaw Mountain, that they have a few men in San Antonio, a sort of outpost."

Jessie nodded. And I'm sure the trouble the railroad had wasn't any secret."

"I wonder now about those other four men Caruthers sent us," Ki said soberly. "It seems to me we'd better start asking a lot of questions, Jessie."

"Oh, I intend to," Jessie assured him. "But let's get the horses in this corral first, before they founder themselves down at the river. And when we've done that, we'll eat and look for those new hands and see what we can find out."

Getting the horses into the rope corral was an easy job, even in the darkness. They were strung out along the riverbank within a space of a few hundred feet. A few of the animals were standing in the shallow water, the others along the bank. Jessie and Ki made short work of getting them into the corral, then started for the fire.

Ed Wright was not among the cowhands hunkered down around the chuckwagon, eating steak and potatoes from tin plates and scooping up chunks of red, juicy tomatoes from the airtights that Gimpy had thoughtfully included in the trail rations. Jessie quickly counted noses. Five of the hands were missing, two from the Circle Star, one from the Box B.

Three of the five who'd been hired in San Antonio: Slaton, Hedley, and Meyers were in the group scattered around the wagon, and Peewee, the young swampy, was tending the fire. The fifth new man, Rader, was not among those having supper. Will Grant was standing beside the chuckwagon, talking to Gimpy between bites.

"Ed's riding the herd," Grant told Jessie when she asked him about the Circle Star foreman. "So's them others that ain't here. They'll start bunching up the steers, then as soon as five of these fellows here has finished their grub, them and me will go spell Ed and them others while they come eat. Don't worry about a thing, Miss Jessie. Me and Ed have got it all worked out."

"I'm not a bit worried, Will," Jessie replied. "Just curious. The remuda's corraled, when you want fresh horses for tonight. Ki and I will eat supper while we wait for Ed."

Jessie and Ki filled their plates and settled down near the chuckwagon. They started supper, watching the new hands while they ate. They saw Grant collect the men and ride off, and a few minutes later, Wright and the crew who'd been gathering the herd rode up and hurried to the chuckwagon.

"Grant must have miscounted," Ki said. "There are only four men with Ed."

"I don't think Ed made a miscount," Jessie said. "My guess is that we've just lost one of our new hands, Ki."

Ki nodded. "Rader. He's the one who's missing."

Holding his filled plate, Wright was looking closely at the eating men, a frown growing on his face. He saw Jessie and Ki and came over to where they were sitting.

"We're short a hand," he said. "Rader. He answered me when I called the men in after Will and his crew relieved us. I don't know what happened, but I just supposed he was following the rest of us in. If he don't get here in a minute or two, I'll ride back to the herd and see what happened to him."

"Save yourself a trip, Ed," Jessie told the Circle Star foreman. "I don't think we'll see Rader again."

"Why?" Wright asked.

"Because he must be the one who rode me down and

knocked me off my horse in front of the remuda just before we got to the river," Jessie replied, and told Wright the details of her experience.

"Are you sure it was Rader?" Wright asked with a frown.

"No. I couldn't see his face," Jessie explained. "Whoever it was had his bandanna pulled up, just like everybody else. All I could see was his eyes and his light-colored Stetson."

"But Rader's missing," Ki pointed out. "And he was one of the new men who came from San Antonio. All we know about them is that Frank Caruthers sent them."

Wright placed his plate on the ground and started to stand up. "You think it's—" he began.

"Yes," Jessie broke in. "It has to be the cartel, Ed."

"How about the other new hands?" Wright asked.

"They haven't done anything so far, and they don't act like they have anything on their minds," Ki said. "Jessie and I have been keeping an eye on them."

"We'll talk to them, of course," Jessie told Wright. "But my guess is that they're what they seem to be. The cartel had time to send Rader when they heard we needed men, but it isn't likely they could move fast enough to plant any more with us."

Wright started to his feet again, saying, "Just the same—"

"No, Ed," Jessie said quickly. "Sit still. Even if we're sure the cartel's at work again, there's nothing we can do now. Rader was the one we needed, but it's too late now. Rader's gone."

Chapter 8

Following the plan they'd worked out while they finished eating, Jessie, Ki, and Wright walked together when they carried their supper plates, cups, and utensils to the chuckwagon. A lantern was hung on the arched slat that supported the wagon's canvas top, and on the tailgate had been placed a dishpan in which the hands could drop their tableware. Peewee, the small, sandy-haired youngster hired as Gimpy's swampy, was busy washing dishes. After Ki and Wright had put their plates and utensils in the pan and moved away, Jessie hung back.

"We haven't had much time to talk since you and the other new men joined the drive," she said to the youth. "How do you like working for the Circle Star so far?"

"Just fine, Miss Jessie." Peewee sloshed a handful of knives through the dishwater and dropped them in the rinsing tub. "It sure is fun, even if I ain't a real cowboy, just a sorta one, right now."

"Is that what you want to be?"

"It sure is! Even if Ma and Pa don't think it's fittin'."

"If they don't approve, how'd they happen to let you take this job?" she asked.

"'Cause we need the money," the youth replied. "Pa's legs won't never be much good again, the doctor says, so I got to help until he gets well and can go back to work again."

"What happened to him?" Jessie asked with genuine concern.

"Oh, he got hurt when he was fixing a locomotive in the San Antone shops. That's why Mr. Caruthers sent a callboy over to the house to tell me I could have this job."

"Your father works for the Southern Pacific?"

"Yes'm. Since before I was born."

"How did Mr. Caruthers find the men who came here with you?"

Peewee frowned and replied, "Why, I don't rightly know, Miss Jessie. Mr. Slaton and Mr. Hedley come into Mr. Caruthers' office while I was talking to him, then Mr. Meyers showed up. Mr. Rader didn't come along until just before we got on the train to start."

"I see," Jessie said. "Well, do your job, Peewee, but if anything comes up that bothers you, come see me and we'll talk about it."

"I like working for Gimpy, Miss Jessie. He's all right. I guess I haven't got nothing to complain about."

Jessie caught up with Ki and Wright, who'd stopped a few paces away during her brief conversation with Peewee. She gave them a brief summary of what the boy had told her, and concluded, "Of course, none of us thought Peewee was involved in what happened to me, but he did give us a lead on who to talk with next."

"Slaton and Hedley?" Ki asked. "They seem to have been chums before they joined us."

Wright nodded. "On the CO, they said. That'd be the Converse spread, out in Arizona, close to Wickenburg."

"Let's see what they have to say, then," Jessie said. She pointed. "Isn't that them right over there?"

Slaton and Hedley were just getting to their feet after finishing their supper when Jessie and Ki and Wright stopped beside them.

"You boys be sure to get a good night's sleep now," Wright told them. "You know we'll be resting the cattle tomorrow, so there's not going to be much to do. But I'll want you to ride night-herd tomorrow night, so make up for the shut-eye you'll miss. We'll be heading the herd out for the Concho the next morning."

"It won't be the first time we've missed a little sleep, Ed," Hedley said. "We've both of us trailed steers before."

"Ed says you're from Arizona," Jessie put in. "It's even drier and hotter there than it is here, from what I've seen."

"It sure is, Miss Jessie," Slaton agreed. "But where we worked was in the foothills of the Hassayampas, so it was pretty green most of the summer. It didn't get too bad except in July, when ever'thing browned over."

"I'd say you jumped out of the frying pan into the fire," Ki commented.

"Well, if you want the dog-bottom truth, we was figurin' to head for the spreads up on the Brazos when we hit Texas," Slaton said. "Except we'd just went busted bucking a monte game in a saloon in San Antone, when some fellow from the SP come in looking for cowhands. When you need a job, you jump at the first one that comes your way."

"I hope you're not sorry," Jessie said. "It's been pretty rough, so far."

"Nothin' we ain't used to, Miss Jessie," Hedley said with a broad grin.

Wright asked, "Either one of you men seen Rader lately?"

"I sure ain't," Slaton said. "Come to think of it, him and Meyers has both been sorta shy about showing up."

"I know where Meyers is," Wright told them. "He's riding the first night-herd stretch."

"Last I seen of Rader, he passed by goin' to the back of the herd quite a ways before we hit the river," Hedley said. "I was riding flank then. Rader told me Grant had put him to ride drag. Didn't seem too tickled about it."

"Well, there's no hurry," Wright said. "I'll run into him after a while."

Walking through the darkness toward the remuda after they'd left the two new hands, Jessie asked Ki and Wright, "Do you think this is shaping up the way we suspected it would? Those two men seemed as straightforward as anyone could expect."

83

"We'd better make sure Meyers hasn't skipped out," Ki said. "If Rader's the only one missing, I wouldn't have any hesitation about pointing the finger at him."

"That's about the way I'd add it up, Ki," Wright agreed.

Jessie said thoughtfully, "I still can't be absolutely sure it was Rader who pushed me, but if he's disappeared, I'm inclined to believe it was him, all right."

"I know we all feel like turning in after the long day we've had, but let's find Meyers, just to make sure he hasn't followed Rader," Ki suggested.

"That strikes me as a good idea," Wright said. "All we've got to do is wait a few minutes when we get between the remuda and the herd. If Meyers is doing his job right, he oughta ride past us before we've waited too long."

"We'll wait, then," Jessie agreed.

Wright's prediction was correct. By the time their eyes had adjusted fully to the gloom away from the fire, the new man came by, riding along the edge of the herd. He was letting his horse set its own easy pace, and when Wright hailed him, Meyers touched the reins and rode over to where the three stood.

"Just taking a look before we turn in," the foreman said.

"It looks all right to me," Meyers reported. "The critters stood the drive right good. All I know about us losing was that one steer that busted a leg."

"That's right," Jessie confirmed. "We came through a lot better than I thought we would."

"This country's not exactly what you're used to, is it, Meyers?" Ki asked.

"It sure ain't like the Archbold spread, or the Klebergs'," the cowhand agreed. "Down there along the Gulf, the winter rains have set in by now. This time of year it'll only rain maybe once a week, but pretty soon it's gonna be rain every day till next summer starts."

"I get the idea that you and rain don't agree," Jessie observed. "Is that why you left?"

"I guess you might say that, Miss Jessie," Meyers replied. "I wasn't too bad off with Archbold, but I guess my

84

feet got itchy. Anyhow, I pulled down my time and left."

"You showed up for us at the right time," she said. "How did you hear we needed men?"

"Why, it was just by accident," Meyers replied. "I was in the Green Front Saloon, and some fellow stuck his head in the batwings and said any cowhand looking for an outfit to tie to oughta go to the SP depot and talk to that Mr. Caruthers. I figured it was worth findin' out about, and when I heard there was a job going with the Circle Star, I was right glad I did."

"Things like that happen," Wright said. "Oh, before I forget to ask you, Meyers, have you run into Rader this evening?"

"Come to think on it, I haven't. I was about in the middle of the chow line, but I don't recall noticing him."

"Well, if you do, tell him I'd like to talk to him," Wright went on. "If you don't see him, I'll run into him later on."

After Meyers had ridden off, Jessie said, "I don't suppose there's any doubt about it being Rader now?"

Ki shook his head. "None at all, Jessie. If it were daylight, I'd be tempted to try to pick up his trail, but by the time I could get started, he'd have covered so much ground that I doubt I could catch up with him."

"He made his move, and it didn't work," Wright said. "By now he's likely cuttin' a shuck back to the Nueces, to report to his bosses."

"And as soon as he's reported, the cartel will find a new spot to attack us," Jessie said soberly.

"They can't do much as long as we're on this cattle drive," Ki pointed out. "By the time Rader gets back and they work up a new scheme, we should have the herd to market."

"Don't forget, Ki, we've still got a lot of miles left to cover," Wright put in. "And we can't move the herd any faster than we're doing now. We're sitting ducks, Ki. There's not any way I know of to hide a herd of steers, and they make a pretty good-sized target."

• • •

After a full day and night of rest, the herd moved well when Wright started the outfit north along Devil's River, in spite of the long, gradual slope they were mounting. It was deceptive country, looking to the eye as though it were level prairie. Its true nature was shown by the riverbed, which now ran in a gorge instead of between low, level banks, and only by looking at the increasing depth of the gorge could the uphill nature of the land be judged.

A day beyond their starting point they reached Dry Devil's River, which lived up to its name. Not even a trickle of water wetted its stony bed. Though a steer broke a leg on the steep, rocky banks as the herd traversed the gorge, and had to be shot, its meat was not wasted. Gimpy dressed it out, then he and Peewee backpacked it up the steep bank to the chuckwagon, and for the next two days the hands fed well on steaks and stew.

"I was gonna hafta butcher a critter anyways," Gimpy told Jessie when she came up to the chuckwagon for supper the night the steer was killed. "We got another week t' go afore we hit the next dry crossin'. When we stop t' rest the herd after we git to the Concho, I'll take the wagon down t' the fort an' stock up at the sutler's."

"How close will we be to Fort Concho?" Jessie asked.

"Oh, not more'n a long day's haul," Gimpy replied. "I was askin' Ed did he figure to give the boys a day t' go into the little town that's sprung up around the fort, but he said no."

"I'm sure Ed has good reasons."

"'Course he does! No smart trail boss is gonna let his hands go off rampagin'! By the time they had a spree an' was able t' do a good day's work agin, we'd lose a week's time."

By the end of the third day after crossing Dry Devil's, the nature of the land began to change. They were nearing the headwaters of Devil's River, though the four or five spring-fed creeks that merged to form the main stream were still a two-day drive ahead. After that, the second of the three wide, waterless stretches the cattle would have to cross lay between the herd and the Concho River.

Though the country they entered now was still arid, it had more graze than the low-level land they were leaving behind. Cactus became scarce and almost vanished. Tall, weedy grass grew in clumps between stretches of stony soil, and day by day these clumps increased both in number and in size; in places the graze stretched in swaths that took the herd an hour or more to cross. The coarse grass was dry, nature's own version of hay, but it grew thicker and taller than did the sparse patches that had sustained the cattle when they'd started from the Nueces.

While the upward tilt of the land was now more pronounced, the herd could move a few miles more each day than had been possible while the trail led through the badly broken terrain they had just left. Because they could now graze each night, the cattle no longer strayed during the hours of darkness in search of something to fill their bellies. This became a bonus for the trail-drive crew, for only two night-herds were necessary, instead of three or four.

"And that's just like adding a couple of new hands," Wright remarked to Jessie and Ki when he came to put the horse he'd been riding during the afternoon with the remuda. "Means all but four of the boys can get a full night's sleep instead of putting in half a night in the saddle."

"It's easier on the horses too," Jessie said. "They don't stamp around and whinny the way they did, so Ki and I can get a little more sleep, too."

"I'll say one thing, Jessie," Wright went on. "That long, dry haul we've got comin' up don't make me boogery, the way the first one did. I know we can do it now."

"How much longer is it, Ed?" Ki asked.

"Close to fifteen miles more than it was from the Nueces to the Devil's, the way I figure it. It'll take two long days and part of another one."

"That's a long way," Ki said thoughtfully. "Won't it be hard on the herd?"

"Sure it will. But if I find there's enough graze when I go to scout it tomorrow, I'll make it as easy as I can. We won't try to make it in one jump. It'll mean two dry camps, but we ought to get to the Concho about the middle of the third day."

"No night drives, then," Jessie said. "That should make the men feel good."

"It makes me feel better, Jessie. When I got a herd moving across strange country in the dark, then's when I start wondering why anybody in his right mind wants to be trailing cattle."

"We've still got another day or two along Devil's River, haven't we?" she asked.

"One full day and a short one, the way I figure it," the Circle Star foreman replied. "And when we get past the headwaters of the Concho, there's just one more long hump ahead, but I'm not worrying about that one until we get a lot closer to it."

After Wright had left to go to his bedroll, Jessie said, "I'll make the night walk tonight, Ki. It's been an easy day, and I'm not a bit sleepy."

"That's fine, if you feel like you need the exercise," Ki replied. "I had a pretty good workout, chasing that walleyed mustang that bolted just before we stopped."

Jessie started her circuit of the rope corral. The moon had not yet set, but a thin, high, broken haze was drifting across the night sky, covering the moon now and then, diminishing its light for several moments at a time. The horses were not as quiet as they usually became at night. The walleyed bronco that had broken away from the remuda a few hours earlier and then led Ki on such a hard chase seemed to have infected the horse herd with some of its restlessness.

As she walked slowly along, Jessie spoke now and then, a word or two in a low, soothing tone. She did not address any of them in particular, but gave them the assurance that horses received from hearing a human voice. Running her hand along the single strand of heavy manila rope stretched in an irregular circle between the chest-high stakes to form a temporary enclosure, Jessie wondered why the horses accepted their confinement within the flimsy corral.

She wished—not for the first time—that she'd been able to bring Sun on the drive. Changing horses in the middle of the day was a necessary move, especially in the rough country they'd been crossing, but it prevented the development of any personal feeling between horse and rider. So far, Jessie hadn't found a horse with which she could establish a bond of communication like that which existed between her and the big palomino.

Jessie's slow circuit brought her to the back of the roughly circular corral. Here the horses seemed even more restless than those at the opposite side of the enclosure had been. Jessie stopped, looking across the backs of the animals, a frown growing on her face. Her instincts were telling her that something was wrong, and after a moment she realized what it was. The remuda did not have the look to which she'd become accustomed, but for a moment the difference did not register. Then Jessie suddenly realized why. Horses that were penned in a small space like the rope corral usually faced in the same direction; tonight she saw as many heads as rumps.

Ahead of where she was standing, one of the mustangs gave a shrill whinny. It was echoed by another in the same area, and all along the perimeter of the enclosure the animals began to stir, turning and stamping the ground, their eyes walling to show white rims. The animals gave no sign of settling down; if anything, they were growing more agitated.

Jessie started walking again, speaking soothing words, straining her eyes through the veiled moonlight, trying to find what was upsetting the horses. The haze that had covered the moon was now drifting slowly away. Turning her back to the remuda, Jessie gazed in the direction toward which the horses had their heads turned. Then the last of the high haze drifted clear of the moon, and her eyes caught a flash of green, a pinpoint of alien luminescence in the grass. The pinpoint moved and another green dot appeared beside it. The moon's face cleared suddenly, and now Jessie saw the panther.

She did not see the animal itself; its long, lithe, tawny body was almost the same color as the grasses among which it crouched. Instead she saw the black shadow of the beast, which the moon's light cast on the tall grass beside it. The panther was not moving, but behind its shadow the grasses were trembling as they were disturbed by its twitching tail.

Behind her the horses began whinnying again—a high-pitched, agitated shrilling. Their hooves were thudding on the hard ground now as they began moving around nervously. Jessie spoke soothing words again, and without taking her eyes off the panther, she brought up her hand to grasp the butt of her Colt. The cougar growled. The whinnying of the mustangs changed into shrill, worried neighs as the big cat's rumbling growls reached their ears.

Jessie had the Colt out of its holster now. She forced herself to move slowly, knowing also that she must aim, rather than merely shoot from the hip. She'd learned long ago that shooting at a moonlighted target was tricky at best. She brought the Colt up inch by inch, her finger curling around the trigger, her thumb on the hammer. But before she could raise the Colt high enough to sight, the panther yowled and launched itself through the air in a mighty spring.

Everything happened at once. Jessie threw caution away. She fired as the animal leaped from its crouch. The leaping cat cried out in midair, its yowl strangely like the shrieking voice of an angry woman. Before Jessie could fire again, she heard the horses behind her breaking into a frenzied mill. Their neighs shrilled louder and their hooves thudded as they surged against the rope barrier. The panther was still hanging in midair, its leap not completed, when the rope corral gave way.

Jessie was directly in the path of the stampede. She got off one more shot at the panther, the arc of its leap declining

now, the beast's snarling fangs only a few yards from her
face. Then the surge of the horse herd enveloped her. She
was pushed to one side, then the other. She tried to keep
on her feet, but one of the horses bumped her off balance.
As Jessie fell, the flailing foreleg of another struck her head,
and then she knew nothing more.

Chapter 9

Ki's voice reached Jessie faintly, as though he were calling her from a great distance.

"Jessie! Are you all right?"

Jessie tried to answer, but the words she formed in her mind came from her mouth in an unintelligible garble. She was sure her eyes were open, but she could see nothing.

His tone even more urgent, Ki called her again. This time he sounded closer to her. "Jessie? Say something!"

Now Jessie could see Ki, a dark form kneeling beside her in the moonlight, his arm around her shoulders, holding her half erect. She tried again to speak, and this time found her voice.

"The panther, Ki!"

"It's lying over there, dead. Are you hurt, Jessie?"

Feeling was coming back to Jessie's arms and legs. She sat up, and Ki helped by lifting her. She looked around, frowning at the confusion of distant voices she heard.

"Are you hurt, Jessie?" Ki asked again, his voice more urgent.

"I—I don't think so."

Jessie moved an arm experimentally, then moved the other arm. Her vision was clearing. She lifted her shoulders free of Ki's encircling arm and sat erect. Her head sagged for a moment, but she raised it and looked around. The voices from the darkness were closer now. She saw her Colt on the ground a foot or so from where she sat, and leaned forward to retrieve it. The gun felt strange, slick with dust, and without thinking she began rubbing her hands over its blued steel frame.

Ki said, "Jessie, count to five for me. Slowly."

His request puzzled her, but she counted as he'd asked her to, and Ki sighed with relief. In a rush, Jessie's memory returned. She looked around. Fifty yards or so away she saw a half-dozen of the horses. They were not bunched, but scattered, dark shapes moving aimlessly in the moonlight, not running now, one or two of them already beginning to graze.

"I'm all right now, Ki," she said. She looked at the dead cat, its eyes no longer glowing green, its body twisted and flattened by the trampling hooves of the bolting horses. "That damned panther jumped before I could shoot it, and spooked the horses."

"Yes. I could tell what happened," Ki replied. "One of them must have knocked you down when they broke out of the corral. You were still unconscious when I got here."

"I remember feeling my head hit something when the horses knocked me down," Jessie said. Moving her head sent a wave of dizziness through her body, and she shuddered momentarily.

Ki asked, "Can you sit here for a minute by yourself, while I try to catch a horse or two?"

"Of course I can, but I don't intend to!" Jessie told him indignantly. She got to her feet, ignoring Ki's outstretched hand. "Get my lariat when you go after yours. We've got to round up the remuda before the horses stray too far."

"You're not going to round up anything," Ki said severely. "The hands are on their way here. They'll get the remuda back in shape. You need to stay in camp until you feel better."

Ed Wright and a half-dozen of the men were within speaking distance now. The Circle Star foreman saw the dead panther and understood at once what had happened.

"One of you boys go get two or three lariats," he snapped. "We'll rope three or four of those closest horses, and get the rest rounded up before they move too far." He turned to Jessie. "It don't look to me like you're hurt. I guess you got in the way when the remuda busted up and bolted?"

"I guess I did," Jessie replied with a wry smile. "The horses must have known that panther was out there a long time before I saw it."

"Sure. You're lucky they didn't trample you."

"You don't have to tell me that, Ed," Jessie answered. "What bothers me most is that my carelessness might hold up the drive. If it does, it's my fault."

"No reason for you to feel that way," Wright replied. "And don't worry, we won't get behind. I was figuring a long day today and a short day tomorrow to get to the place where we'll cut off over to the Concho. We'll just make it a short day today and a long one tomorrow. If you feel like riding, that is."

"I feel perfectly all right," Jessie assured him. "I don't quite feel like helping you and the boys round up the horses, but I'm going up to the chuckwagon now to tell Gimpy to make a pot of coffee for the men when they come in. And whenever you want to start driving tomorrow, I'll be ready!"

As Ed Wright had promised, the breakup of the remuda by the panther did not delay them. Before sunrise on the third morning after the big cat's aborted attack, the hands began driving the steers across the more than forty miles of barren prairie that lay between the last brooks which flowed into Devil's River and the first tiny tributaries that merged to form the Concho. Wright had already scouted the route they would follow, and his report to Jessie on his return had been optimistic.

"There's pretty good grass all the way across," he'd said. "Same kind the steers been feeding on since we hit Devil's River. It's a lot drier than what they've been getting, but it'll hold enough dew in the mornings so they won't miss water too bad."

"There aren't any water holes, then?"

"Nary a one. A few draws, but they're bone dry."

"You're sure we can make it in three days, Ed?"

"Easy enough. I figure to hit the Concho about noon on the third day. We'll rest the herd a day then. That'll give Gimpy time to take the chuckwagon down to Fort Concho. He's runnin' low on supplies, so he'll get enough from the sutler's store there to carry us to the prairie towns up north."

With the sun in their faces, the cattle plodded at an even pace across the sea of grass that stretched to the flat horizon. It was a treeless, featureless landscape. Once the low, rocky bluffs that dominated the terrain west of Devil's River had dropped from sight below the horizon behind them, there was nothing to break the sky in any direction they might look.

Only the rippling tips of the tall grass, which grew as high as the knee joints of the steers, told them they were not riding across a sandy desert. In the morning when they started, the grass was soft and pliant from the dew that had collected on the stalks. Though the drops of dew clung only to the surfaces of the grass stems, the moisture softened them enough to make them resilient; they bent readily and sprang erect as the herd passed.

By early afternoon, as the heat of the sun began to increase in the cloudless sky, the grass dried quickly. By midafternoon it no longer snapped erect as the animals trampled through it. After they dried, the stems snapped and broke, and until sunset their trail showed as a wide, uneven swath.

When the drive started the next morning, the cattle showed no ill effects from the lack of water. The steers maintained a steady pace, plodding patiently, but by midafternoon they began to grow restless. Here and there one stopped, then another, and the herd began to spread. The flankers were kept busy, weaving into the mass of slowly moving animals and prodding the laggards to move on with the others. The remuda did not suffer; horses have only one stomach, and do not need the quantities of water required to keep the four stomachs of cattle functioning properly.

Still, the herd kept up a steady advance as the sun dropped behind it and dipped toward afternoon. There were still three hours or more of daylight left when Ki noticed the haze that was growing on the eastern horizon.

"Maybe we won't have to worry about water, Jessie," he said, pointing to the soft gray haze. "That cloudbank rolling in might bring rain with it."

Jessie glanced cursorily at the hazy horizon and shrugged. "Perhaps you're right, but I don't think it'll rain at this time of the year."

They'd ridden for perhaps another half-mile when she looked at the sky again and exclaimed sharply, "That's not a cloudbank, Ki! That's smoke! There's a prairie fire burning ahead of us!"

Ki studied the horizon for a moment. "You're right," he agreed. "I hope Ed's noticed it by now!"

"We can't take a chance, Ki," Jessie said. "You'll have to handle the remuda by yourself while I ride up and tell him."

Spurring around the slow-moving herd, Jessie found that Wright had already seen the haze and had also identified it as smoke. His voice sober, the Circle Star foreman said, "I've got to turn the herd north right away, Jessie, before they get a whiff of that smoke. Once they smell it, the steers will go crazy, and that fire's moving fast and spreading, too."

"Can we get clear of it before it reaches us?"

"I'm betting we can," Wright replied grimly. "And that's one bet I don't aim to lose."

"Do you want Ki and me to help the men?"

"Not now. They can handle it. Just keep the remuda as close behind the cattle as you can. Don't forget, horses panic too, when they smell smoke."

97

With a wave of her hand and a nod, Jessie wheeled her pony and rode back to the remuda. She could see the shift in the direction the cattle were moving soon after she left Wright. The point men at the leading corner on the right were slanting north instead of northeast, while the flankers on the right-hand side of the herd were pulling away, encouraging the animals to spread in that direction.

At the same time, the flankers on the left side were pushing the steers, forcing them to stay in a compact mass, and at the back of the herd the drag men were duplicating the moves made by the point riders, crowding the steers on the left side to move faster, while giving those on the right plenty of space to make room for them. Since the front of the herd, when it was on the move, extended for almost three-quarters of a mile, and its mass spread behind the lead lines for nearly two miles, the maneuver ordered by Wright took more than an hour to complete.

Jessie sighed with relief when the change of direction had been made and the remuda was following the steers almost due north. She'd glanced at the line of smoke several times while she and Ki were hazing the horse herd to follow the steers in swinging around the quarter-circle, and each time she'd looked, the smoke was billowing higher and in a denser cloud over the tan prairie grass.

Now, with the herd's new route established and the remuda in its usual place, following the steers, she looked again. The flames themselves were visible now, an angry red line flickering along the surface of the ground, under dense billows of gray smoke rolling and rising high into the sky. The line of flame was not much more than four to five miles from the herd now, Jessie estimated, and she wondered if it was her imagination, or if the fire was creeping forward faster than it had earlier.

Looking across the backs of the horses, she could see Ki. He had turned in his saddle and was watching the line of fire as it crept toward them. Jessie waved, but Ki's attention was on the approaching blaze. She glanced at the

98

horses again. They were moving calmly enough. She toed her horse into a canter and circled behind the animals, pulling up beside Ki.

"What do you think?" she asked as she reined in her mount to match Ki's pace.

"I think we're in trouble," Ki said soberly. "The fire's gaining on us. It won't be long now before the animals start smelling smoke. Look."

Jessie followed his pointing finger. The smoke rising from the long line of flames seemed denser than it had been even a few minutes earlier. It was beginning to wisp at the top now, small tendrils of gray shooting above the mass of the smoke in winding fingers that were carried forward by the easterly breeze toward the moving cattle.

Wetting a finger in her mouth, Jessie held it up. The left side of her finger dried quickly, leaving the right side still moist.

"Of course!" she exclaimed. "The fire's making its own wind now! It has to, in order to keep burning! The heat's pulling the wind along the ground toward it!"

"Are you sure?" Ki frowned.

"Certainly I am! That's something my father taught me! You know how much time he spent at sea, Ki, and the sea's where he learned about winds and weather."

"I suppose you're right, then," Ki replied. "For all the good it does to know something like that."

"But don't you see?" Jessie asked excitedly. "With the ground wind blowing toward the fire, we can set backfires, and that'll stop the big fire from spreading!"

"But I still—" Ki began.

Jessie did not wait for him to finish. "Watch the remuda for a few minutes by yourself, Ki," she said. "I'm going to ride up and tell Ed we'd better start backfires right away!"

Jessie was spurring her horse before she finished speaking. She galloped between the edge of the herd and the flames, only a bit more than a mile distant now. The cattle were already starting to act nervous as the reversed wind at ground level brought an occasional whiff of smoke to their noses.

As she drew close to the head of the herd, Jessie could see for the first time the width of the wall of fire creeping toward them. It stretched for nearly two miles beyond the line of the lead steers, and was rolling implacably toward them. Ed Wright was at the lead corner of the herd, talking to Possum, who was riding point. Both men were watching the line of fire. Jessie reined in and called to the Circle Star foreman.

"Backfires, Ed!" she said. "We've got to set backfires along the line of the fire! That'll stop it from reaching us!"

Wright stared at her for a moment, then his eyes widened. "Sure!" he exclaimed. "I'm a damned slow-thinking fool, Jessie! All I've been able to think about is a way to get the herd moving faster than the fire! Come on! Let's go get Gimpy!"

"I'll do that," Jessie said. She realized she was taking the command from her foreman, but time was too precious to waste at that moment. "You pull off the extra flankers and the spare drag man and have them ready by the time I get back with the torches. We don't have any time to waste!"

Like all chuckwagons, Gimpy's carried a bit of everything that might be needed on a trail drive. The cook produced empty gunnysacks that had held potatoes and beans, a coil of flexible wire he used in securing anything that could not be held together with rope, and, most important, boxes of matches and a five-gallon can of coal oil for the lanterns. The can was only half-full, but that was far more than would be needed to soak the strips of gunnysack that Jessie and her crew would use to start the backfires.

While Gimpy cut the gunnysacks into strips with his big butcher knife, Jessie twisted lengths of wire around one end of the strips, leaving enough extra wire to allow the strips to be fastened quickly to the end of a lariat and as quickly removed. The whole job was done in less than a half hour, and by the time Jessie returned to the herd, Wright had

100

pulled Mossy, Tom, Cujo, and Archer from their positions with the herd and was waiting for her when she rode up.

Quickly she explained her plan to the men clustered around her, then began dividing the dripping, smelly strips of fabric among the four men, handing each of them a handful of matches at the same time.

"We've got to get as close to the line of fire as we can," she went on. "I think the wind will be blowing away from us when we're inside of a quarter of a mile from the flames. We'll split up when we leave the herd. Archer, you and Tom and I will ride for the north end of the fire. Cujo, you and Mossy go in the other direction."

"Excuse me, Miss Jessie," Archer said. "How you expect us to start a fire with these little hunks of gunnysack?"

"Wrap the wire around the end of your lariat," Jessie said. "When you're a quarter-mile from the fire line, throw an open loop in your rope, light the sacking, and let it drag ten feet or so behind your horse while you ride parallel to the fire. Don't ride fast, give the grass time to catch. When the first piece of gunnysack burns up, put on a new one and keep going."

"Sounds easy enough," Cujo said, shrugging. "Let us go and do it, no?"

"It might not be as easy as it sounds," Jessie warned. She was standing in her stirrups, looking at the long line of fire. Remembering the prairie saying that a rider on horseback could see no more than seven miles to the horizon, she estimated the line of fire to be more than ten miles long. She went on, "Keep your distance from the men on both sides of you. I'll be in the middle. Watch me for signals. Now, if everybody understands what you're to do, let's ride!"

They galloped toward the line of flame, fanning out as they rode. Jessie watched them as best she could, trusting to her horse to keep out of trouble. The air grew warmer as she got closer to the blaze, and now she could feel the backdraft sweeping across her face. Before she was within

101

the quarter-mile from the line of flames she'd specified, the air was almost too hot to breathe and the horse was shying away. She checked the animal with the reins and pulled her bandanna up to cover her nose and mouth.

Looking at the others, Jessie saw that they were stopping too. She took her lariat from its saddlestring and attached one of the oily strips of sacking to its end. The wire bent readily. Then she followed her own instructions, paid out ten or fifteen feet of loop, and touched a match to the sacking. It blazed up faster than she'd anticipated, and she had to drop the burning fabric quickly.

When the blazing cloth hit the ground beside its hooves, Jessie's pony jumped ahead, but she held her seat in the saddle and pulled the animal to a halt. The jump had put the strip of burning cloth behind her, and around it the grass was already starting to burn. She toed the horse ahead, looking over her shoulder at the line of flame she was creating. The freshly kindled blaze was creeping slowly toward the wildfire, fanned by the backdraft.

Jessie sighed with relief when she saw that her plan had a chance of working. She held the horse on a tight rein, forcing it to move forward at a walk. The air that enveloped her grew hotter, and sweat was soon dripping off her face, but she could ignore that when she looked back along the fire line and saw the black patches of burned grass growing larger in advance of the wildfire, reducing the earth to a bare, charred surface and consuming the fuel the wildfire required to keep spreading.

When Jessie had covered almost two hundred yards from her starting point, the piece of gunnysack she was dragging disintegrated. She reined in and took hold of the wire that had held the first strip, but pulled her fingers away with a start when she touched the tip of the hot wire. She wrapped on a new strip of gunnysack, lighted it, and started riding again.

After that, it became a matter of stopping when necessary to replace the burned-up sacking, ignoring the punishing heat and the painful blisters that swelled up on her fingertips from her incautious hurry to replace the first strip. Ahead of her and behind her, Jessie saw the others doing their jobs in the same methodical way she was doing hers. The backfires that had been set first were meeting the wildfire now, and the flames of both were dying away.

Finally she reached the point where Tom had started his backfire. She could see him and Archer ahead. Both were close to the ends of the strips along which they'd been working; behind her, Cujo and Mossy were already finished and riding up to join her. Jessie was turning her head to look north again when a vagrant eddy swept the air in front of her clear of smoke.

In the narrow strip of clear air created by the swirling wind, Jessie saw a rider across the area of black. The man was staring at her just as she stared at him, and with a shock Jessie recognized him. The man on the other side of the burned strip was the missing Rader.

Chapter 10

Jessie grabbed her Winchester from its saddle scabbard. She flinched when her hand closed around it; she'd forgotten about the painful blisters on her fingers. She ignored the pain and lifted the rifle. She saw Rader belatedly reaching for his own rifle as she brought her Winchester to her shoulder. Then, before she could settle the rifle against her shoulder and get Rader in her sights, the smoke hid him again.

Jessie was still sitting immobile, her rifle shouldered, when the crack of a shot sounded through the eye-defeating smoke and she heard the angry whine of a rifle slug zipping past, a few inches from her head. She ducked instinctively and kicked her horse forward. Another shot from beyond the wall of smoke missed her by a dozen yards. Cujo rode up.

"Somebody shoot for you, Miss Jessie!" he exclaimed.

"Rader," Jessie said tersely. She knew that no further explanation was needed. Rader's disappearance after his effort to unseat her had been a topic of discussion among the hands, though the men were unaware of the cartel connection. "He's on the other side of the burn."

"Don' worry!" Cujo said. "I fix him okay!"

"No, Cujo!" Jessie cried, but she spoke too late to stop Cujo from wheeling his horse and spurring for the blackened strip. "The ground is still too hot!"

Before Jessie had finished her warning, Cujo's horse gave him the same message. The animal started into the burn, then whinnied unhappily as smoke filled its nostrils and its hooves hit the hot ground. In spite of Cujo's heavy hand on the reins, the mustang kept bucking and dancing sideways until it had left the burned-over area. Cujo stayed in the saddle, and once the horse was out of the smoke and felt cooler ground underfoot, it stopped rearing and stood shivering in the aftermath of its panic.

"I tried to tell you," Jessie said to Cujo. "The horses won't cross the burn until it cools and stops smoking."

"Theen we ride to the end and go around, no?" Cujo asked.

Jessie did not reply for a moment. She had swung around in her saddle to check the progress the herd had made. Though the low-hanging sun was in her eyes, she could see the herd and the men tending it in silhouette, and as far as she could tell, they were having no problems. The cattle seemed to have settled down and were plodding ahead, still moving parallel to the burned area, the remuda following the steers.

Turning back to Cujo, she said, "Let's see if we can get around the end of the burn before Rader gets away. I've got an idea that he set this fire!"

"This man is got bad *rencor* for you, Miss Jessie," Cujo said. "Better we get him as wait till he do something else."

Mossy rode up. "Who done that shooting?" he called as soon as he was within earshot. He saw Jessie's rifle in her hands. "Was it you, Miss Jessie?"

"No. It was Rader. He's on the other side of the burn."

"We go to get him," Cujo told Mossy. *"Andamos, amigos!"*

The smoke that still curled from the wide black strip veiled what lay on the other side; the three men spurred their mounts toward the place where the fire had stopped. Tom and Archer joined them as they passed, and the group quickly covered the distance that remained to the end of the burn. They turned and rode around the end of the blackened, still-smoking area. On the east side of the burn lay only empty prairie. Rader had vanished.

"Sangre de la Virgen!" Cujo breathed, his voice solemn. "Thees Rader, he ees *brujo!*"

Jessie shook her head. "No, Cujo. He's not a magician or a witch. He's just found someplace to hide that we can't see."

"We find him, then!" Cujo said.

"We'll look," Jessie agreed. She glanced at the sun again. "We don't have too much time, it'll be dark pretty soon, but let's scatter and see if we can't flush him out."

While the men spread out and began riding in slow zig-zags, seeking Rader's hiding place, Jessie rode back to the burn. She was sure Rader had set the prairie fire, but she had no proof. Knowing the way the cartel operated, Jessie did not need to have Rader's orders spelled out for her. She knew the cartel kept spies watching the Circle Star, and she was positive that when word had reached the cartel's bosses that the herd would be driven to market instead of shipped by rail, its leaders had given Rader a blanket order to harass and try to destroy the cattle any way he could. His attack on her had been one move, the fire was another, and unless he was captured or killed, she was sure he would attack again.

Scanning the ground as she rode slowly along, Jessie soon found what she'd been looking for. To anyone else, her find might have been meaningless; it was nothing more than an empty box that had contained wooden matches, but the box was new, not yet soiled and stained by weather. Obviously it had not lain on the prairie very long. Jessie did not bother to pick up the box. There was no way to connect it with Rader, but to her it told its own story of him riding along, dropping bundles of six or eight burning matches every few yards until the prairie was ablaze.

Two rifle shots from the direction of the herd drew Jessie's attention just as she was riding to join the men who were looking for Rader. She turned to look, and saw Ed Wright sitting on his horse a dozen yards in front of the herd, waving his rifle above his head after firing to attract her attention. The sun was touching the western horizon now, and Jessie realized that the time had come to give up their search for Rader. She looked around; the men had heard the shots and seen Wright's signal, and were riding slowly toward her. She rode to join the men.

"He is noplace, Miss Jessie," Cujo told her. "Like I tell you, this Rader, he is *brujo*."

"No, Cujo," Jessie said. "He's just outsmarted us this time by getting away. But he didn't do us any real harm, and now that we know he's around, we'll catch him the next time he shows his face."

"I couldn't figure out what you and the boys were doing," Ed Wright told Jessie as she and the firefighting crew rode up. "Hope I didn't upset nothing."

"You didn't, Ed," Jessie replied. "We were looking for Rader, but we weren't having any luck finding him."

"Rader?" Wright exclaimed. "You mean he—"

"He set the prairie fire," Jessie said. "Come on and ride back to the remuda with me, and I'll tell you and Ki about it at the same time, while the herd's being bedded down for the night."

"We won't be bedding down," Wright said. "That's why I signaled you to come back. I need the men here to help work the steers tonight."

"You mean we're not going to cross to the Concho?" Jessie asked as they started toward the rear of the slowly moving herd.

"No," Wright said. "After I saw how much grass that fire burned up, and figured how big a loop we'd have to make to get to the Concho, it looked to me like the best thing to do is drive straight on north to Mustang Draw."

Jessie rode in silence for a moment, then she said, "I know you've worked everything out by now, Ed, but I'll ask you just one question. Are you absolutely sure we can make it safely?"

"You mean to Mustang Draw?" Jessie nodded and Wright went on, "I'm as sure as a man can be sure of anything anymore, Jessie. By the time we zigzag to the Concho around that burn, and double back on our trail coming north again, we'll cover about the same number of miles it'll take to get us to Mustang Draw. Same number of days, too. I can't see any difference."

"We know there's water in the Concho River, Ed. Can we be sure there'll be water in the draw?"

"That far south, Mustang Draw drains two more draws," Wright replied. "And there's creeks to the east of it that we can make, if push comes to shove."

"What about Gimpy's supplies?"

"He says he can squeeze us through. We might be on short rations for a day or two, but after that we ought to be okay."

"All right then," Jessie agreed. "It's Mustang Draw."

By this time they'd reached the remuda, and Jessie told Ki and Wright how she'd seen Rader on the east side of the burn, about the shots he'd fired and the matchbox she'd discovered.

"It's too bad he got away," Ki commented after her account was finished. "But we know now that we've got to keep a sharper watch."

"I'll see to that," Wright said. "Night's when we need to be extra careful. I'll put on another night-herd, once we get to Mustang Draw. There won't be a lot of sleep for any of us till we hit water again."

Wright's prediction proved to be correct. Although the herd traveled no greater distance, the continuous driving and the lack of water took a serious toll. The first night passed without incident. The cattle kept their usual pace, but late that day and through the night they moved more and more slowly. As they'd done on the all-night drive from the Nueces to Devil's River, the steers lagged and began trying to leave the herd in search of water.

By sundown of the following day, with another full day and part of a night ahead before the drive would reach Mustang Draw, men, horses, and cattle alike were bone-tired and out of sorts. The men nodded in the saddle, their usually keen attention and quick responses becoming ragged. The horses sensed the relaxing of their riders' control and lazed along. The herd was even more seriously affected. Much more than the men or the horses, the cattle depended on water, rest, and food—in that order—and they had been the first to be deprived of all three. The herd began to break up.

Ed Wright did not become aware of the breakup until it was far advanced. Worried when the cattle had started straggling and she'd seen no action taken by the Circle Star foreman, Jessie left Ki to handle the remuda and spurred ahead on a fresh horse to see what was wrong. She found Wright dozing in the saddle while his tiring horse plodded along.

"Ed!" she called. "Wake up! We're getting into trouble!"

Wright's head snapped up and he pulled himself erect. "How do you mean, Jessie?"

"Look back at the herd and you'll see."

Turning in his saddle, Wright looked back through red-rimmed eyes. He saw that the herd was no longer a tightly packed entity, but many small, spaced-out bunches, some moving, some standing still with their heads drooping listlessly, a few lone steers wandering between the separate bunches.

"Oh, God, Jessie!" he exclaimed. "I'm sorry! Not that it helps much to say that."

"You don't need to say anything, or apologize either, Ed," Jessie said. "I know you've been changing horses every three hours and going without rest since we left Devil's River."

"That's still no excuse," Wright said, tight-lipped. "I'd better get busy! Look at that mess!"

He waved his hand in a sweeping gesture that took in the entire herd. The point men were riding wide of the herd's lead steers, the flankers lagging to the rear, the drag men swaying in the dust, with their eyes closed. Even the remuda looked ragged, the horses strung out in a loose line instead of being in their usual compact mass. As he leaned forward to grasp the reins that he'd let sag over his pony's neck, Wright's stomach wrenched and twisted and he almost toppled from his saddle.

"You're going to eat something before you do anything with the herd," Jessie told him firmly. "Come on. We'll ride up to the chuckwagon together."

They rode side by side to the chuckwagon, which was rolling a few hundred yards in advance of the cattle herd. Gimpy was nodding on the wagon seat, Peewee curled up on the supply box behind him. Jessie leaned down and called to the cook.

"Gimpy! Wake up! Ed's got to have a bite to eat!"

Blinking himself awake, Gimpy said, "It ain't gonna be much, Miss Jessie. I ain't had no chance t' do what I'd oughta been at. We been rollin' too much."

"Do what you can," Jessie said. "And I'd sure like a swallow or two of coffee, if you've got any."

"Yep, you look like you need somethin'," Gimpy agreed. He twisted in the seat and shook Peewee. While the youth was yawning into wakefulness, Gimpy looked back at the steers for the first time. "Gawdamighty!" he gasped. "The herd's bustin' up! Damned if we ain't in a big mess o' trouble, Ed."

"You don't have to tell me that," Wright said. "I've got to get waked up enough to get the hands moving again. We could lose half the herd or more if we don't chouse the critters along to Mustang Draw without wasting any more time."

"Them hands needs vittles, Ed," Gimpy said. Peewee at last responded to Gimpy's prodding and sat up, rubbing his eyes. "Git Ed an' Miss Jessie a biscuit apiece, and one o'

111

them cold steaks and a cup o' that coffee outa the bucket, younker," Gimpy told the kid. And you better take a swallow o' coffee yerself. We got work t' do, real fast."

Gimpy hauled on the reins and the team stopped at once. Even though he was still only half awake, Peewee thrust biscuits and thin-cut fried steaks into the hands of Jessie and Wright, and a moment later gave them each a cup of cold coffee before he jumped out to chock the chuckwagon's wheels.

Gimpy crawled into the back of the wagon and squatted down in the narrow aisle between the compartments that filled most of its bed. He opened one of the compartments and began rummaging in it while he talked.

"Now lissen to me, you two," the old man said sternly. "I reckon I've likely made more trail drives than either one o' you ever will. I know what them hands needs t' perk 'em up an git 'em over this hump. How much more o' this leg's left t' go?"

"Tonight and tomorrow. Part of tomorrow night, too, I'm afraid," Wright replied, after swallowing the bite of biscuit he'd been chewing. He followed it with a sip of the cold coffee. "This sure hits the spot, Gimpy," he said.

"I'm sure all the hands would like a bite, Gimpy," Jessie said. "Can you do the same thing for them that you've done for us?"

"I ain't got but a few biscuits left," Gimpy said. "Plenty o' them little steaks, though. But if you don't mind me buttin' in, I'll fix th' hands up so's they kin make it t' Mustang Draw."

"How can you do that, Gimpy?" Jessie frowned.

"I'd like to know too," Wright said quickly. "The hands are beat to a man. So am I, so are the steers and the horses."

"I can't he'p you with the critters, but if the men's all right, they'll push the critters through," Gimpy said. He was pulling tin cans out of the compartment as he spoke. "I aimed t' save these airtights fer a blowout the night afore we hit Dodge, but we need 'em worse right now than we will then."

112

Wright looked at the labels on the cans and whistled. "You really splurged, didn't you, Gimpy? Peaches!"

"They're hard t' find and precious high-priced," Gimpy said. "But they'll save yer bacon right now, if y'll do like I say."

"Go on," Jessie told the old cook. "We're listening."

"Y'll need all the men t'night. Now, what you need t' do is send the men up t' eat right now. I got enough o' them cold steaks cooked up t' go 'round, and when they've et 'em, I'll hand them peaches around. Soon as the hands is done eatin', you git 'em started shaping the herd. I don't know what they put in them airtights with the peaches, but it'll work on them men like a big shot o' whiskey, an' they'll work hard an' move fast agin."

"Now hold on, Gimpy!" Wright protested. "I don't want my hands drunk when they're chousing steers!"

"Wait, Ed," Jessie broke in. "Let Gimpy finish."

"I wasn't meanin' they'd be drunk, Ed," the cook explained. "Jes' feelin' good agin, ready t' work."

Gimpy took one of the tin cans and sliced two cuts in the shape of an X in its top with his cleaver. He poured half the peaches into each of two tin cups, put spoons in the cups, and handed them to Jessie and the foreman.

"Now put these in yer bellies whilst y' listen t' me," he said soberly. "Soon as the men've et their peaches, git the herd shaped up an' movin' fast. Come daybreak, send half yer hands ahead t' find me and th' wagon. I'll have grub fer 'em, and see they git in their bedrolls soon as they've et. Time you come up with th' herd, the hands that's slept kin push it on 'thout stoppin', and the rest kin sleep a-while."

"Wait a minute!" Wright protested. "Once we get the herd shaped up, I guess I can get by with half the crew tonight. The steers are going to be in worse shape tomorrow night than they are now, though, and it'll take every man I've got to handle them then!"

"I know that! I'll see they git rousted out their rolls in time t' catch up with you by sundown tomorrow, an' finish pushin' the herd t' Mustang Draw."

"How can they work the way you say they will?" Jessie frowned. "These peaches don't taste any different from others I've eaten out of airtights. What's in these besides peaches?"

"I don't know as there's anything special in 'em, Miss Jessie," Gimpy said. "It don't seem t' matter who put up the airtights, anyhow. I got a hunch why it works, though. Either one of you ever eat a whole half-airtight of peaches before?"

"No," Jessie said slowly. "I don't think I ever have."

Wright frowned and shook his head. "Me either. They cost so much, I usually throw in with two or three other fellows and split one between us."

"Sure," Gimpy nodded. "That's about four little hunks o' peach and a swallow o' juice apiece. Leastwise, that's what Brad Close tells me t' do at th' Box B, and he ain't no different from any other owner I ever worked fer."

"It's not because owners are stingy, Gimpy," Jessie said quickly. "I know peaches in airtights are expensive, but they're hard to find. We can't always buy enough to go around if the men were to get a half-can apiece."

"Sure. I know that, Miss Jessie," Gimpy replied. "But just the same, I'd give a pretty t' find out why they steam a man up so good. I can't figure why, but when peaches in airtights was right new, I stumbled onto the way they boost up a man when he feels like he can't go no more. Saved *my* bacon a couple o' times, too."

"All right," Wright promised. "I'll do what you've told me to, Gimpy. But God help us all, and especially Jessie, if this scheme of yours doesn't work!"

"Don't worry about me, Ed," Jessie said. "We all know the Circle Star stands to lose a lot of cattle if Gimpy's scheme doesn't work, but what's important is to get our men back in shape. They'll do their jobs, if we give them what they need."

Much to Wright's surprise, and to the surprise of Jessie

114

and Ki, to whom Jessie revealed Gimpy's secret, the canned peaches restored the men's vigor. They shaped up the herd in the dying hours of the day, and got it started toward Mustang Draw just before darkness fell. The herd moved much more slowly than it had before, and now and again one of the animals would lurch to its knees and fall over, and lie still after the herd had passed. There were relatively few that gave up, though. The steers complained with unhappy blatting, but the herd instinct would not allow them to stop. Through the long hours of the brilliant moonlit night, the revived hands kept the cattle moving.

A breakfast of flapjacks and syrup and ham revived the tired men when the herd reached the chuckwagon. Following Gimpy's instructions, Wright did not let the cattle stop. The hands ate in shifts, and half of them stayed behind to sleep while the rest of the crew kept the cattle forging ahead through the morning, and when the sleep-refreshed men who'd stayed behind at the chuckwagon took over, the drive kept moving without a pause.

At dusk, though Mustang Draw was still more than an hour's drive away, the cattle smelled the water and started moving faster. The full crew was back at work before they reached the draw, and for two hours all hands were kept busy chousing the thirsty animals out of the shallow, brackish water and onto the grass to keep them from drinking too much and foundering.

Jessie stood beside Ki on the bank of the draw, watching the herd as it settled down for the night. She said quietly, "This time last night, I'd written off half the herd as a loss, Ki. I was angry with myself for ever agreeing to make this trail drive. Now I've changed my mind."

"I'm surprised we lost so few," Ki said. "How many head were missing when Ed made the tally?"

"Only sixteen. Ten from the Circle Star herd, six from the Box B. And right now I'd bet any amount that we're going to get the rest of the herd safely to Dodge City, even if the cartel does keep on trying to stop us!"

★

Chapter 11

"Not that I ain't glad for your company, Ki, but there's not much real need in you coming along," Ed Wright said. "Seems to me like you're doing enough riding every day so's you wouldn't relish any extra."

Ki and Wright had slowed their horses to a walk as they mounted one of the long upslopes of the rolling prairie that lay between Lost Draw and Beale's Branch of the Colorado. After resting at Mustang Draw following the prairie fire, the herd had moved north along Lost Draw, which lay roughly north and south and drained into Mustang Draw. If the scouting trip they were now making showed that Beale's Branch of the Colorado held water, it would be the next stop, then the cattle would be driven due north to the main branch of the Colorado.

Ki swept his hand around in a gesture that embraced the endless expanse of prairie, its yellowing grasses bright in the late-morning sunshine. "I suppose I just wanted to take a look at the country without having a bunch of mustangs along," he replied. "But I haven't had a chance before to go with you when you've been scouting, and I'm curious to know what you look for."

"Not much of anything except the best route for the herd to take. Along here, it don't make a lot of difference. In real dry country, like the part we just left, it might make a lot."

"We don't have many more dry drives to make now, do we?"

"Nothing like the ones we've been through," Wright said. "The maps don't show any more, but maps ain't always right. Now, you take Beale's Branch, it's not even on some maps, so I figure I'd best come and make sure it's there."

"What if it isn't? Or if it's dry?"

"Then we'll head north instead of east and push on to the main fork of the Colorado. But if we do that, we'll need to make a real early start when we leave Lost Draw, and move fast instead of lazying along like I'm hoping we can."

"This drive is a lot longer than I'd realized," Ki said. "You know, Ed, traveling on trains most of the time, the way Jessie and I do, we forget how big this country is, and how slow a herd of cattle moves."

"I sorta forget it myself," Wright smiled. "And that can be—" He stopped short and reined in, shading his eyes with his hand while he peered ahead. "Looks like we're fixing to run into company up ahead. Unless I'm badly mistaken, that's an emigrant wagon I see."

Following Wright's pointing finger with his eyes, Ki said, "Yes. And it's not moving. They must be having trouble."

"We'd better go find out," Wright said, reining his horse in the direction of the wagon.

They rode toward the canvas-topped wagon, and as they drew closer, Ki said, "They're in some sort of trouble, all right, Ed. There are two women moving around the wagon, but so far I haven't seen a man."

"We'll find out soon enough, I guess."

When Ki and Wright had gotten within hailing distance, one of the women standing beside the wagon called, "Are we glad to see you men! We've been hoping somebody would come along this way since right after sunup!"

"What's your trouble?" Wright asked as he and Ki reined in and dismounted.

"Two broken spokes on that back wheel of the wagon,"

the woman said, pointing. She went on, "I'm Sarah Folwell, and this is my sister, Amy."

"I'm Ed Wright, and this is Ki," Wright said. "We're from a trail herd that's heading north. We came out to scout the route we'll be driving over tomorrow."

Ki studied the two women unobtrusively, letting Wright do the talking. Each had dark blond hair caught up with a ribbon at the neckline, and blue eyes, high cheekbones, and an oval chin. Their noses were thin, with high-arched nostrils; both had full, generous lips, and as far as Ki could tell by glancing at their loose gingham dresses, their bodies were sturdy and well-rounded. There was a difference of several years in their ages. From the worry-lines in Sarah's face, Ki judged her to be the eldest; Amy's face was smooth and clear. He noticed that both wore wedding rings.

"We're trying to make it down to the Big Bend country," Amy volunteered. "But Sarah's husband was taken sick— he's asleep in the wagon now—so the two of us have been handling the team."

"We heard something crack last night," Sarah said. "It was when we crossed a river a ways back. This morning, a little while after we started, something else popped and the wagon commenced wabbling, so we stopped. That wheel looks awful bad, and we were afraid it'd get worse if we kept on going."

"Let's have a look," Wright said.

He and Ki walked to the rear of the wagon, the women following them. Ki glanced around once and saw the pair examining him with their foreheads puckered in puzzled frowns. He was used to being stared at, especially in sparsely settled sections of the country—his appearance *was* unusual. Many people assumed he was Chinese, but he was often mistaken for an Indian or a Mexican, with his almond-shaped eyes, his long, straight, pure black hair, and his sallow complexion. His clothing was remarkable as well, contrasting strongly with the ranch-country garb customarily worn by men in the West. He favored loose-fitting apparel that would allow the sort of mobility he needed when his special talents were called upon: a collarless, white cotton blouse; a scuffed, well-worn black leather vest with many pockets; a pair of rope-soled, black cotton slippers. The only parts of his clothing that were commonplace were a pair of frayed denim trousers, a red bandanna, and an ancient, disreputable-looking black Stetson. At the moment, of course, both he and Ed Wright were covered with a patina of yellow trail dust that somewhat muted the contrast between their clothing and complexions.

Wright hunkered down to examine the wheel at close range. Ki joined him. One of the spokes was broken into two pieces, and another was badly cracked. The wheel was bulging ominously.

"It sure needs fixing, no two ways about that," Wright said. "A few more miles and that wheel's going to break up."

"We were afraid it couldn't be fixed at all," Sarah Folwell sighed. "And we've just got to keep going. Joe needs a doctor."

Ki had been examining the wheel. "If you've got a few tools and a straight piece of wood, we can splice these broken spokes," he told them. "It's not a big job, but the wagon's going to have to be raised. I hope you've got a jack."

Sarah shook her head. "I'm afraid we haven't. We've got an ax, a saw, a hammer, and a wheel-wrench in the wagon, if that helps any."

"We can make do," Wright said. "Ki, let's unhitch the team and use the wagon tongue for a lever. We'll find a few rocks to prop up the axle while we're working on the wheel."

"We'll help all we can," Amy offered. "Won't we, Sarah?"

"Of course. I just wish Joe was able to help, but he's real sick. It's his stomach. He ate some meat I think was spoiled, and he's had diarrhea and been vomiting. He's still awful weak and wobbly on his feet."

"You ladies think you can unhitch the team while Ki and me get some big rocks?" Wright asked.

"Of course we can!" Sarah said. "Come on, Amy."

Ki and Wright began searching for rocks, not easily found on the grassy prairie, but after ranging around a few minutes they discovered a good supply in a dry creekbed and hauled what they needed to the wagon. The horses had been unhitched, and taking off the long sturdy oak wagon tongue was a simple job.

Setting up one pile of rocks behind the axle where the tongue could be used as a lever, and a second pile of rocks to hold the wheel off the ground so it could be removed, Ki and Wright put their weight and muscle on the end of the wagon tongue and raised the axle the few inches needed to allow Sarah to slip a final rock under it. They let the wagon down slowly and stepped back to inspect their work.

Amy and Sarah joined them. After they'd stood silently for a moment, looking at the tilted wagon and its broken wheel, Amy asked, "What do you want Sarah and me to do?"

"We'll be needing your wheel-wrench and saw, and if you've got some spare harness leather, we'll want that," Wright said. "I guess if we need anything more, we'll just ask you when the time comes."

"Don't be bashful about asking us, now," Sarah told them. "I'm going to have to sit with Joe a little while, but Amy'll be here, and if you need me, you just call out."

"I'll get the tools and leather you want," Amy said. "It'll just take me a minute or two."

When the women had gone, Wright said, "This ain't gonna be a quick job, Ki. It's gonna take a while to get that wheel off, and we'll have to saw a strip of wood off the seat to use for splints. Wrap them with harness straps, they'll hold."

"That was the way I figured to do it," Ki agreed. "You're right, though. It'll take some time."

"Thing is, I'm responsible for Jessie's herd," Wright said, frowning. "I oughta be heading back. Will Grant won't know where to stop for the night unless I give him the lay of the land we've scouted. These ladies said they had to ford a stream late yesterday. That'd be Beale's Draw, and there's water in it, so that's the main thing I needed to know."

"If you're asking whether I can handle the repair job alone, Ed, the answer is yes," Ki said. "There's no reason for both of us to stay. Start back whenever you want to."

"If you're sure you won't need me to help . . ."

"I'm sure. If I do, the ladies can lend a hand. If it's too late for me to ride back when I've finished fixing the wheel, I'll just stay here and join the drive when you get here with the herd tomorrow."

"That's the best thing to do, I guess," Ed said. "I'll explain things to the ladies and be on my way, then."

When Wright had left, Ki started work. After putting a two-foot length of harness strap to soak in a pan of water, Ki removed the wagon wheel with the wrench Amy found for him, and rolled it to a level spot where he could force the spokes into alignment. Then he sawed strips of close-grained birch from the wagon seat to use for splints. While he was working, he glanced into the wagon and saw Sarah sitting beside her husband, holding his hand. Joe Folwell's eyes were closed, his face pale.

"How is he?" Ki asked.

"Some better, I think," she whispered. "I gave him a dose of laudanum. He's about asleep, he'll sleep till morning."

"I'm sorry he's sick," Ki said. "You stay with him. Your sister and I will manage." Ki went back to where the wheel lay and fished the strap out of the water. Drawing his *tanto* from the sheath at his waist, he told Amy, "If you'll hold the leather strap for me, we'll cut it into strips now."

"That's a funny-looking knife," Amy said, looking at the *tanto*'s slim, curved blade. "I've never seen one like it before."

"It's Japanese," Ki told her.

122

"Are you from Japan, then?"

"I was born there." Ki did not mention that his father had been an American and his mother Japanese; he saw no reason to go into a discussion of his ancestry. "But I've lived in this country many years."

"And you're a cowboy?"

He smiled. "Sometimes."

"You don't dress like they do, though."

"No. I like my own style of clothing better."

"It does look comfortable."

"It is," Ki assured her. "Now, if you'll hold one end of this harness strap, I'll cut it."

Amy grasped the end of the strap and held it up dangling in the air. "Like this?" she asked.

"No. Flat on the seat." Ki took her hand to show her how to place the strap and hold it with her fingertips. He felt her muscles tighten when he was arranging her fingertips, and asked, "Is something wrong?"

She shook her head. "No. Go on, cut the strap."

Ki divided the piece of leather into narrow strips with deft strokes of the curved blade of his *tanto*. Its keen edge slipped through the softened leather like it was butter. Amy followed him to the wheel, and watched while Ki arranged the narrow pieces of birch to cover the cracked place in the least-damaged spoke. He started winding the strip of leather around the splints, but could not hold the splints firmly in position and wind the strip on at the same time.

"You'll have to help me, if you don't mind," he told Amy.

"That's what I'm here for," she said. "Show me just how you want to hold them."

Ki took her hands and arranged them on the splints. Again he felt the involuntary twitching of her muscles when he touched her, but this time he did not ask any questions. He wound the strips in a double-diamond pattern around the splints, pulling them tight, stretching the wet leather, and securing the ends with a serpentine knot. Then he mended

123

the other spoke in the same fashion, and stepped back to look at the finished job.

"There!" he said. "The leather will shrink as it dries and will hold the splints tight. You'll have to take it easy until you get to a blacksmith shop and have new spokes put in, though."

"We will," she promised, then asked, "Are we going to put the wheel back on now?"

Ki looked at the sky. Dusk was gathering. He said, "We'd better, while the light's still good. But we'll leave the wagon on the rocks until the leather's dry."

While they were lifting the wheel to put it back on its axle, Sarah came out. "I didn't expect you'd be finished so soon," she said. "I'd have been fixing supper, if I'd known."

"If Ki doesn't need me now, I'll help you," Amy offered.

"You stay and help him," Sarah said. "I can manage. It's not going to be much, just ham and potatoes, and it's no trouble to get a few sticks of wood out of the possumbelly."

"That sounds good to me," Ki told her. "We'll be through in just a few more minutes."

Supper was a quiet meal, Sarah's mind obviously on her sick husband, and Amy did most of the talking. The three were from Arkansas, and had started across Texas from the Red River ferry crossing on its eastern border almost a month ago, heading for the Big Bend, where Joe Folwell had a cousin who had written about the cheap land that was available there. Until Joe's illness, they'd made good progress, and now that he seemed to be getting better, they hoped to reach their destination in another three weeks.

Sarah excused herself early, saying to Amy, "I'll put your bedding and a groundcloth and blanket for Ki on the seat, where you can get them when you're ready for bed."

"I've been sleeping under the wagon," Amy explained. "It's too crowded for three in the wagon bed."

Ki stood up. "It's been a long day for me," he said. "And

124

for you too, I'm sure. I'll just take my bedding now and go off to one side and turn in, if you don't mind."

Walking what he considered a respectable distance from the wagon, Ki spread the groundcloth and blanket, and folded his vest for a pillow. Removing the *surushin* he was wearing as a belt, he loosened the waistband of his trousers for comfort and lay down. He'd almost dropped off to sleep when he heard the soft rustling of feet in the tall course grass. Ki sat up and looked around, but in the faint starshine all that he could see was a shadowy figure walking toward him.

"It's me, Ki," Amy said. Her voice was low and strained. She stopped beside the blanket and stood looking down at him, her face in dark shadow, her figure outlined vaguely against the sky. "I—it's—well, if you don't want me to stay, I'll—"

"Stay, Amy," Ki said softly. He threw back the blanket he'd pulled over himself. "Come on, lie down. I'm glad you came to me, because—well, you know why I couldn't come to you."

"I know," she said, stretching out beside him. "But I could tell when our hands touched while we were working—" She broke off and groped for Ki's hand. "Touch me, Ki! I want to feel your hands on me." She took the hand she was holding and pressed it to her breast.

Ki rubbed her breasts softly with his sensitive hands, feeling her nipples harden under his touch. He raised himself, bent over, and found her lips with his. Amy inhaled in a gasping sigh and thrust her tongue into his mouth. Her hands slipped down his chest, found the loosened waistband of his trousers, and slid inside. Ki felt her warm fingers fondling him. He began to grow erect.

Amy broke their kiss to gasp, "Oh, Ki! It's been such a long time since I've been with a man!"

"Your husband?" Ki asked softly. "I noticed your ring."

"It doesn't mean anything. My husband died more than a year ago, and I've been—well, lonely's not enough to

125

describe it. I haven't been with a man since then."

Amy started tugging at Ki's waistband, trying to pull down his trousers. He raised his hips and she yanked them down to his knees; then before Ki could move, she'd lifted her dress and straddled him and was guiding his stiff member into her.

Ki lay quietly, letting Amy do as she wished. She began to rock her hips back and forth, her face turned to the sky, her breath bubbling in a string of low-pitched groans. He'd been in her for only a minute or two when her hips and torso erupted into a writhing frenzy and her moans became low screams.

Amy covered her mouth with her hand and continued to rock back and forth until she exploded into another spasm. This one was not as violent as the first, but it lasted longer. When at last she was still, she sank down with her head on Ki's shoulder and sighed contentedly.

"I'm sorry, Ki," she whispered after a moment of silence. "I just couldn't wait to go through the polite motions. I didn't even take off my dress, but I will now." She raised herself erect and whipped the dress over her head, then said, "You must think I'm terrible, but I don't care a bit, I feel so good."

"I don't think you're terrible at all," Ki assured her. "I never have believed that a woman has to hold back and wait for a man."

"I'm glad you said that," Amy told him, "because I'm ready to start all over again. I feel you inside me, and I think you might be ready too."

Ki responded by cupping her full, firm breasts in his hands and caressing their protruding tips. Amy leaned forward and he began nibbling their firm tips with his lips. She shuddered and sighed, and moved her hips suggestively. Ki clasped his arms around her and, without withdrawing, rolled her onto her back. Then he began stroking, slowly at first, then faster and more forcefully, until Amy started bringing her hips up to meet his vigorous thrusts, little cries

126

of pleasure escaping her lips as their bodies met.

"Oh, Ki, don't ever stop!" she whispered. "Even if I let go again, don't stop!"

"I don't intend to stop," Ki told her. "Let go when you want to. The night's just starting, and we won't waste a minute of it."

When false dawn brightened in a thin line along the eastern horizon, Amy kissed Ki goodbye and slipped back to her own bed.

"Sarah will be up in a little while," she said. "And we'll be moving on. But I'll never forget you, Ki. You've given me something I'll remember all my life."

Later, when the sun was just showing its rim, Ki stood watching the wagon rolling away. He watched until it dipped into one of the little hollows that marked the prairie here and there, then folded his knees and sat down where his blankets had been spread during the night. Patiently he waited for the arrival of the herd.

★

Chapter 12

"Chouse 'em to the water, boys!" Ed Wright shouted at the top of his voice, calling to the hands across the Colorado. "You might as well get used to it, because we've got a lot more rivers to cross before we hit Dodge!"

For their first real river crossing, Jessie and Ki had left the remuda in the rope corral and joined the hands to help get the steers across the stream. Jessie had been sitting her mount at the water's edge on the south bank. On hearing Wright's command, she toed the horse into the river. It picked its way daintily through the unfamiliar element, and Jessie grew a bit tense as well.

After a moment the animal settled down, and Jessie discovered that the bottom shelved so gradually that the animal was only a bit more than fetlock-deep when she reached her station twenty feet from shore. She lost the apprehension that she always felt when entering a strange river, though Wright had told her, after he'd zigzagged back and forth across the stream, that the bottom was hard and clean.

Ki was already at his station in midstream, in deeper water, though even there the river was not quite belly-deep to his horse. Jessie followed his example and freed her lariat from its saddlestring. She shook the rope into a small loop, and closed her hand around the eye to keep the loop from growing larger. From the shore she heard the shouts of the hands as they obeyed Wright's order to start the cattle moving.

Now the Circle S foreman reined his horse into the water. He stopped a dozen yards from the north bank and stared at the herd with an anxious frown as the cattle drew closer to the river's edge. In response to some strange instinct that no cattleman really understood, when a steer tried to break from the herd during a river crossing, it invariably moved with the current, so no riders were needed on the upstream side of the path the herd would take while crossing.

An easy day's drive from Beale's Branch had brought them to the Colorado with plenty of time to cross the river before dark. Scouting the stream's banks the day before, Wright had found the remains of a dozen long-dead cooking fires. The old campsites, marked by weathered, scattered coals, were all the evidence he'd needed to choose the spot found safe for crossing by drivers of the longhorn herds of years gone by.

After their long rest following the detour they'd made to escape the prairie fire, two nights and a day spent at Mustang Draw, the cattle had made only the short, easy drives from the draw to Beale's Branch and from there to the Colorado. The herd was once more in good condition; in fact, the steers and the remuda were in better shape than the men tending them, for the chuckwagon's supplies had been exhausted, and meals had been scanty indeed. Gimpy had cooked the hands their last real meal on the evening they reached Mustang Draw.

When the big Sharps .50s of the hide-hunters had knocked down the last of the buffalo, the hide-towns where Gimpy planned to replenish their food supplies had died as well. They'd seen mute evidence of the departure of both even before they got to Mustang Draw: white, scattered buffalo bones and the skewed stakes which had supported the buffalo-hide-covered shanties that gave the little settlements their name.

The long detour forced on them by the fire that Rader

had set removed any chance of replenishing food supplies at Fort Concho, so the men had lived on an all-meat diet. Gimpy's feast of flapjacks and syrup and ham after the blowout on peaches had been the last full meal the old cook had been able to prepare.

Strong coffee might have helped the constipated hands to digest the fried steaks they ate twice a day, but Gimpy was now counting each individual coffee bean that he used in the hand-cranked grinder. The pale yellow brew he produced drew unflattering comments from men whose stomachs and intestines remained clogged with half-digested meat even after long minutes of squatting and straining over the latrine trench.

"I ain't even got enough pepper and salt t' season the damn meat right," Gimpy had confided to Wright. "Nor no castor oil t' he'p the ones that got the worst gut-gripes. When're we gonna hit a place t' buy the grub we need t' finish out, Ed?"

"Not for another week, Gimpy. The biggest hide-town here on the Llano Estacado used to be up on the headwaters of the Brazos, a place called Buffalo Springs, and I've heard it's still there. That's what I'm gambling on, anyhow."

"Well, I don't know what kinda odds yer buckin', Ed," the old cook growled. "But I sure hope y' got a winner."

In slightly different language, Jessie had expressed the same hope to the Circle Star foreman. "Would it be better for us to wait here while Gimpy and Peewee go back to Fort Concho and buy supplies, Ed?" she'd asked.

"I don't think so, Jessie. The men aren't starving, or even hungry. They can tough it out a few days, until we get across the Colorado and up along the Brazos."

"I'm sure you're right, Ed, but I'll admit I'm getting tired myself of having nothing but steak for every meal."

"We'll only have one long dry drive to make the rest of the way, and that'll be right after we cross the Colorado. Then we'll just ease on along the Double Mountain Fork of the Brazos for a couple of days until we get to Buffalo

Springs. I'm sure Gimpy can buy fresh supplies there. Don't you think we can go that much longer eating steak without it hurting us?"

"Oh, I'm sure we can. It's not like having no food at all, but I know we'll be glad when we can have something else."

Jessie watched the first steers approach. The men had compressed the animals in the front part of the herd into a long, tight column. From where Jessie sat, the herd looked like a bottle with a long neck pointing toward her. Behind the lead animals, it bulged into a rough circle. The flankers who were spaced closely on each side at the front kept chousing the cattle in the bulge to pack tightly, so that only a small part of the herd would be in the water at one time.

In spite of the width of the bulge at the rear of the herd, there was only one man riding drag. The rest of the hands were strung along the flanks to keep the cattle packed closely and to force them into the narrow column in a tight formation.

When the lead steers entered the water, they stopped and lowered their heads to drink. The point men swung their lariats, and the ropes whistled through the air and landed on the rumps of the animals that had hesitated. With short, unhappy blats, they started moving ahead once more.

Jessie found she had very little to do as the cattle moved slowly past. Although the flankers rode only a few yards into the river after the column of cattle had entered the water, and then turned to gallop back to the rear and help the men narrow the bulge, the steers rarely broke their formation before reaching her. That close to the bank, the animals were just getting the feel of the strange element they were encountering, and kept moving forward with very little spreading out.

In midstream, Ki had a more difficult time. The cattle had grown used to the idea of wading by the time they reached him, and though the current was gentle, a few responded to its tugging and veered away from the column, trying to wander downstream. Ki was kept busy riding back and forth, swinging the looped lariat to shy a steer back into position before it got too far from its fellows.

On the opposite bank of the river, Wright confined his attention to the cattle that were in the water. The steers' legs were much shorter than those of the horses, and in midstream the water came several inches up on their chests and bellies. The farther the steers got across the stream, the greater became their tendency to respond to the pressure of the current against them, and to angle downriver. Wright was kept moving constantly, hazing the animals in the proper direction.

Once they'd reached the Colorado's north bank, the steers began spreading out, but they grazed as they moved, and would be easy to form into a herd again when all of the animals had crossed and the full crew had followed them. That job would not be done until morning, after the steers had grazed off and on during the hours of darkness and all the hands except the night-herders had gotten a full night's sleep.

Darkness was almost full by the time the last of the cattle had crossed and the remuda was driven over to join them. Jessie and Ki were late in reaching the chuckwagon. The hands had been served and were hunkered down in twos and threes around the dying cookfire before Jessie and Ki arrived. They'd gotten their thin steaks and pale coffee and were walking away from the wagon when Wright rode up and dismounted. He took his plate and cup and followed Jessie and Ki to the fire. The three sat down.

"Well, we got 'em across nice and clean," the foreman said with a sigh of satisfaction.

"It was a good crossing, Ed," Jessie agreed.

"We couldn't have asked for a better one," Ki added.

"I figure to let everybody rest tonight," Wright said. "The steers won't scatter too much, they'll bunch along the river for the most part, and it's an easy day's drive tomorrow to the Double Mountain Fork."

"I hope you're right about that town you called Buffalo

Springs still being up there," Jessie said. "The boys haven't complained too much, but I'm sure they'll be as glad as I will to see beans and potatoes and biscuits again."

"Even after we hit the river tomorrow, we'll have to drive alongside of it for three more days before we get to the town," Wright said. "The last I heard, Buffalo Springs was still the biggest hide-town in these parts."

Jessie said wryly, "But it's still a four-day drive, you said. That's four days more of eating steaks, but I suppose we can last that long."

Wright grinned. "I suppose we'll have to, Jessie. The next closest place where we'd be able to find any kind of store is Tascosa, and we're still a long ways from there."

"We're about two weeks away, aren't we?" Ki asked.

"Give or take a day, depending on the kind of luck we have." Wright put his plate down, his steak only half eaten. He stood up. "I'll put in with you on being tired of steak, Jessie, and all of us wanting a change. I don't suppose you'd mind if we laid over a day when we hit Buffalo Springs?"

"No, of course not, Ed. The men have earned a day off. If any of them need money, let me know. Just be sure they stay out of trouble."

"Oh, I'll keep a tight rein on them. Well, I'm heading for my bedroll. Tomorrow we'll have a real short drive, but before we start, we've got half a morning's work gathering the herd."

As Wright had predicted, Buffalo Springs had grown into a town. Before stopping, the Circle Star foreman led the herd in a wide circle around the little settlement and two miles past it to Black Water Draw. As soon as she and Ki had gotten the remuda settled down, Jessie's curiosity prompted her to ride the short distance into town for a quick look at the settlement.

Riding down its wide main street, she saw at once that Buffalo Springs still bore the distinctive marks of its origins.

Though most of the houses and all of the stores and saloons that lined its main street were constructed of lumber, she estimated that about a third of its residents still lived in hide houses left standing from the buffalo days that had ended only a few years earlier. Here and there on the street she saw an occasional grizzled character whose beard, as shaggy as the outside walls of the hide houses, spoke of buffalo days.

Hide houses were not architectural dreams; they were made by driving tall, sturdy poles in the ground in a square or rectangle, and nailing buffalo hides to them. The hides were the air-dried kind called "flints" by buffalo hunters. While still warm from the buffalo's body, the hides had been scraped well on the flesh side, rubbed with arsenic to prevent ants and other insects from eating them, then stretched flat and staked on the prairie with the hair side down and allowed to dry.

After a week under the broiling sun, the flints hardened until they were as stiff as boards and almost as thick. Building a hide shack was a half-day job. For walls, hides were sawed into rectangles and nailed, hair side out, to the framework of supporting poles. On two sides, the tops of the walls were sawed at a slant, an angle that would allow the roof to shed rain, more hides nailed to wide-spaced rafters to form the roof.

An opening was cut for a door in one side, and perhaps a single window in the opposite wall, and the dirt inside the shack tamped down hard. The durability of hide shacks was attested to by the fact that as primitive as they were, those in Buffalo Springs were still being lived in several years after the buffalo had been hunted to the verge of extinction.

Somehow the sight of the houses and hunters, relics of the past, depressed Jessie. After riding the length of the main street and assuring herself that Gimpy would have no trouble getting the food and supplies he needed, and that the hands would have all the outlets they wanted to discharge their accumulated yearnings for a blowout, she rode back to the herd.

"I'm splitting the men into two shifts. I'll let half of 'em go in and blow off steam while the other half tend to the critters," Wright told Jessie when she returned.

"I was sure you would, Ed. That's why I rode in. I wanted a quick look at the place before the boys blow its lid off."

"If you and Ki want to go in, one of the men who'll be staying here can keep an eye on the remuda."

Jessie shook her head. "No, thanks. Ki may want to go, but I've seen enough of Buffalo Springs to satisfy my curiosity. When things settle down, I'll wander up the draw until a find a quiet spot where the bushes are high, and take a bath. After that, I think I'll be satisfied just doing nothing for a while."

Anxious to get to town, the men worked faster than usual. In less than an hour they worked the steers into a herd again, and shortly after Jessie and Ki had finished the rope corral and penned up the remuda, the hands who'd drawn the first trip into Buffalo Springs were ready to depart.

"Are you sure you don't want to go in and take another look at the town?" Ki asked Jessie.

"Very sure indeed, Ki. But don't let that stop you from going. I'll keep an eye on the horses."

"No, you go have your bath before the sun goes down. It'd be difficult for you to bathe after dark. I'll join the next bunch when they go in," Ki said. "The glimpse I got of the place when we passed it aroused my curiosity."

"I hope you're not disappointed," Jessie told him. "But if you're going, I'd better have my bath right now. Spit-baths with a washrag and a bucket of water only take the trail dust off, and my hair could stand a real washing."

Carrying a towel, a bar of soap, and fresh clothes from her saddlebag, Jessie walked along the bank of the draw until she reached a thick stand of mesquite several hundred yards from the herd. The brush grew thick to the water's edge, and the lapping of the water against the shore had

136

scoured away the earth bank between some of the bushes that were partly rooted into the draw. Despite the draw's name, its water in the little indentations was glass-clear. Looking into it, Jessie could count the tiny pebbles that covered the bottom.

She found a cove where the brush was thick enough to screen her from the eyes of the hands tending herd. Unbuckling her gunbelt, Jessie hung it on a convenient branch of one of the mesquite bushes. Slipping out of her boots and trail-stained clothes, Jessie hung them and her towel and fresh garments beside the Colt. With the soap in her hand, she stepped into the clear water. It was cool and very shallow, little more than ankle-deep.

Looking along the shore of the draw to make sure she was not visible from the camp, Jessie took a short step into deeper water. The pebbles on the bottom hurt her feet, and she scuffed them back and forth to make a clear space to stand. Her movement roiled the water and she stood for a moment, waiting for it to clear again. The brush behind her hid the camp and the town, and she gazed idly across the draw.

Beyond the line of brush that lined the opposite shore, there was nothing except the rolling prairie that stretched to the horizon in low billowing humps no higher than the lapping of ocean waves on a windless day. The featureless landscape offered only grass and sky, and held Jessie's attention for only a few moments. She looked down at her feet to see how the water was clearing, and just as her eyes left the prairie vista, a glint of sunlight flashed at ground level.

Jessie's brow furrowed in a frown as she looked at the thin beam of light. She stared at the spot where the speck of light originated, but saw no movement. In a few moments the glitter vanished.

After a moment of thought, Jessie decided that the glint of light could only have been created by a piece of glass, probably a whiskey bottle discarded on the prairie by some camper or traveler. The glass, she thought, must act as a reflector for only the few instants that the sun was at a certain precise angle, and vanish as the sun continued its orbit. She dismissed the phenomenon, lowered herself down into the water, and began bathing.

Walking back to the herd, the dying sun warm on her back, Jessie began thinking of supper. She looked around for the chuckwagon, but it was not in its usual place to the north of the herd. Ki was just outside the rope corral, tightening the cinch of his saddle.

"I thought you'd be in town by now," Jessie said.

"I would have been, but the first bunch that went took their time coming back to camp, and Ed rode in to stir them up. He asked me to stay and keep an eye on things until Will Grant got here, and Will rode in just a few minutes ago."

"What happened to Gimpy? He and Peewee should have been back with the chuckwagon a long time ago."

"My guess is that Gimpy stopped at a saloon after he bought the supplies, and just lost track of time," Ki replied. "Most of the hands will eat in town, anyhow."

"I'm getting hungry." Jessie frowned. "I suppose if I want any supper, I'm going to have to change my mind and go in with you, Ki."

"That's a fine idea, Jessie. While you're saddling up, I'll go ask Will to have one of the men who's had his fling keep an eye on the horses, and we'll ride in and eat. And while we're there, we'll look for Gimpy and send him back. If he's drunk, he'll have plenty of time to sober up before he cooks breakfast."

A few minutes later Jessie and Ki set out, heading for the lights of Buffalo Springs, which were already gleaming through the gathering darkness.

Chapter 13

"It looks as though Buffalo Springs is just hitting its stride for the night," Ki remarked as he and Jessie rode down the main street.

"It's busy, all right," she agreed, looking at the men crowding the board sidewalks, their shadows stretching half-way across the wide, unpaved street as they passed through the pools of yellow lamplight spilling from the doors of the stores and the saloons' batwings. "We'd better stop at the first restaurant we see, Ki. I imagine they'll all be about the same, but I'd rather eat before we begin looking for Gimpy."

"So would I," Ki agreed. "And it's a long time since I've been as hungry as I am right now. Supper first, then."

Only two items were chalked on the menu slate at the little restaurant they entered: stew and steak. Jessie and Ki had no trouble making a choice. The stew was surprisingly tasty, thick with carrots and potatoes as well as chunks of meat in a gravy heavily flavored with canned tomatoes.

Their hunger appeased, they moved on down the street, Ki walking, going into each saloon, while Jessie rode and led his horse. They stopped at four of the bars before Ki came out supporting the missing cook. Gimpy's legs were rubbery, his eyes open but glazed, and he was babbling incoherently. He sagged against Ki as they stood on the board sidewalk, not fully aware of his surroundings or who was holding him up.

"He's really drunk," Ki said. "I don't think he knows who I am or where he is, and I can't understand his mumbling."

"Peewee wasn't with him?" Jessie asked, frowning. "No. And nobody has seen him. The barkeep said that when he came on duty over an hour ago, Gimpy was just where I found him, sitting up asleep at a back table by himself."

"He must have taken on a really big load," Jessie said. "And we certainly can't leave here until we've found the chuckwagon."

"I've asked him where it is, Jessie, but all he can do is mumble some gibberish I can't understand."

"Have you looked in his pockets, Ki? When I told him the names of the two or three places that looked like they could fill out the list of things he wanted, I reminded him to be sure to get a receipt."

"Let's hope he bought them before he started drinking," Ki said, beginning to rummage through Gimpy's pockets. He produced a sheet of yellow ledger paper and said, "Good! This is the receipt. It's from Barkum's Store, wherever that is."

"I don't remember noticing their sign on the way in," Jessie said. "Let's go on to the end of the street. If we don't see it, we'll know we've passed it and backtrack."

With Jessie still in the saddle and Ki maneuvering Gimpy along the sidewalk, they moved ahead slowly. They'd almost reached the end of the street, and only three or four lighted doors still showed in front of them, when Jessie called, "Just ahead of you Ki! There's a sign that says Barkum's Store, but the place is dark, and the chuckwagon isn't out in front of it."

"We'll have a look anyway," Ki replied. "There might be a back door that—"

A staccato burst of gunshots interrupted him. There were two reports that both Jessie and Ki identified instantly as having come from a large-caliber pistol, followed by two higher-pitched shots from smaller-caliber guns. Then a third shot sounded from the heavier weapon, and three men came running from a dark passage, an alley apparently, that opened on the far side of Barkum's Store.

Jessie drew her Colt, but as she leveled it at the backs of the fleeing men, the thought came to her that she didn't know who they were or why they were running. She held her fire, but called for them to stop. They ignored her and went on. Ki let Gimpy sag to the sidewalk and started into the dark passage that ran alongside the store. Jessie swung out of her saddle and followed him.

A shot greeted Ki as he rounded the back corner of the store building. He dropped to the ground and rolled, and as he moved he recognized the chuckwagon, standing beside a large building at the side of the store itself. Jessie reached the corner of the store and stopped, her revolver leveled. After a moment she also recognized the chuckwagon.

"Peewee?" she called. "Was that you shooting?"

"Miss Jessie?" the youthful swampy replied. His voice was not quite trembling, but was filled with anxiety.

"Yes. And that's Ki on the ground."

"I thought maybe it was after I let off that shot, but I wasn't sure," Peewee said. "I'm sure glad I missed!"

"Not half as glad as I am," Ki said, getting to his feet.

"What in the world's going on here?" Jessie asked as she joined Ki in walking toward the chuckwagon.

"I wish I could tell you that, Miss Jessie," Peewee said. "From what I heard 'em say while they was coming toward me, them men I run off was about to steal the chuckwagon."

"Steal the chuckwagon?" Jessie echoed as she and Ki reached the wagon. The young swampy's face was white in the gloom, his eyes as round as silver dollars.

"Yes'm. And I didn't know what to do, except I remembered Gimpy kept his gun under the seat." Peewee held up the pistol, a heavy old Colt Dragoon. "I jest hauled it out and blazed away. Only this big old gun's got a kick like a mule, and I didn't hit none of 'em."

"And you don't know who they were?" Ki asked.

"I couldn't rightly see 'em, it was so dark," Peewee said. "Except that one of 'em sounded to me like the man Gimpy went off with for a drink of whiskey. But that was a long time before dark, and he still ain't come back."

"Don't worry about Gimpy," Jessie told the youth. "Ki and I found him in a saloon up the street. He was so drunk that he couldn't talk plainly, and we began looking for the chuckwagon."

"Maybe you'd better start from the beginning and tell us everything just as it happened," Ki suggested.

"Sure," Peewee replied. "We was waitin' in the store whilst they loaded up the wagon when this man come in. He took one look at Gimpy, and said they used to work on the same ranch, a long time ago. Gimpy didn't seem to remember him, but the other man was real sure, and he asked Gimpy to go have a drink. Gimpy told me to stay with the wagon and not leave it till he got back, so that's what I done. Shouldn't I oughta have, Miss Jessie?"

"Of course you should have, Peewee," Jessie said. "You did exactly the right thing."

"I know I waited an awful long time," the swampy went on. "I got real hungry, but I dasn't leave, 'cause Gimpy said somebody might steal what we'd bought if one of us didn't stay here and guard it. I was afraid if I went looking for him—"

"You showed good judgment," Jessie broke in. "But about the man who said he was an old friend of Gimpy's— you hadn't seen him before, I suppose?"

"No, Miss Jessie. And the way Gimpy talked, he hadn't either. But the man kept asking him to have a drink, so after a while, Gimpy said he would."

Ki said, "Jessie, it's going to be a long time before Gimpy can tell us what happened to him. We don't have a chance in the world of finding those three men who ran away. Suppose we put Gimpy in the wagon, let Peewee drive it, and we'll ride back to camp with them."

"I was thinking the same thing," Jessie replied. "Peewee, you can drive the chuckwagon, can't you?"

"Sure, Miss Jessie. I take the reins on long hauls when Gimpy needs to have a nap."

"Give Ki a hand getting Gimpy in the wagon, then, and we'll start back," Jessie said. "We'll get his story from him in the morning at breakfast."

Riding back to Black Water Draw in the black velvet night, Jessie asked Ki, "Do you smell the same rat I do in the story Peewee told us?"

"I'm sure I do," Ki answered. "Rader and the cartel. He'd know the route we're taking. We never tried to keep it a secret from the men."

"Yes," Jessie said. "I don't think we need any more proof that he's a cartel operative. First the fire, now this."

"I suppose you've checked the book," Ki said.

"Of course," Jessie replied. "But you know it wouldn't tell us anything unless he was using his real name, and even then only if he was fairly high up in the cartel, which I don't think he is."

The book to which Ki had referred was a black-leather-covered manuscript book that Jessie always carried in her saddlebags. It was a hand-copied, condensed version of a larger book kept in a secret drawer of Jessie's father's desk back at the Circle Star. The book contained the names and short biographies of cartel operatives around the world. Alex Starbuck had begun to compile the book many years ago, and Jessie had continued to add to its entries since his death.

"He'd know how badly we'd be crippled if we lost the chuckwagon, of course," Ki said. "Traveling alone, he'd have had plenty of time to get to Buffalo Springs several days ago and hire a few of the plug-uglies who always hang around a town."

"I'm sure we haven't seen the last of him, either. We both know the cartel's men don't give up easily."

"Do you have any ideas, Jessie?" Ki asked. "Because right this minute, I don't see any way that we can protect ourselves from any more unpleasant surprises they might pull on us."

"I don't have any more ideas than you do, Ki. But I

think we'd better say as little as possible to the hands about what we suspect. As far as they're concerned, Gimpy met an old friend and got drunk with him."

"Yes, that's sensible," Ki agreed. "I'm not worried about Ed and our own men from the Circle Star, but the Box B hands might get edgy."

"We're still a long way from Dodge," Jessie went on. "Two more weeks on the trail, perhaps three. But even if we can't keep them from striking again, I'm sure of one thing. Whatever the cartel might try, they're not going to stop us from getting this herd to Dodge City!"

"We oughta get to Running Water Draw in plenty of time to get the herd across tonight," Ed Wright told Jessie as he reined in beside her and pulled up his horse to match the gait of hers. "It's one of the shortest pushes we'll make, and the critters and hands are both fresh after that layover in Buffalo Springs."

"Speaking of the layover, did Gimpy say anything to you this morning?" Jessie asked.

Wright shook his head. "Nothing except how sorry he was. I didn't push him too hard, but I guess you noticed I kept him with the herd today instead of sending him on ahead."

"I wondered about that," Jessie said. "Of course, on such a short drive, he'll have time to get supper ready while the boys are forming up the herd for the night."

"I sorta figured you could visit with him while he's fixing supper," Wright said. "He'd be likelier to talk to you than he would to me."

"I'll see what I can find out," Jessie said. "At breakfast he apologized to me and promised it wouldn't happen again, and I let it go at that. He'll get around to talking about it, as soon as the embarrassment wears off a bit."

Gimpy had been on the job that morning when Jessie and Ki went to the chuckwagon for breakfast, but he'd avoided talking to them. The herd had started soon after daybreak, and had made good time over the flat, featureless country during the day. Wright looked at the sun, hanging just above the horizon.

"I'm aiming to push the boys to get the herd on the other side of the draw before we stop," he told Jessie. "Even if it means working in the dark."

"Wouldn't that be dangerous? If the steers should break away, we'd lose a lot of time rounding them up."

"They won't break," Wright said confidently. "Don't forget, draws ain't like rivers, Jessie. They're standing water. Even Running Water Draw's not really running water. I won't worry none, because there's no current to make the steers try to turn. You wait and see, they'll amble across as pretty as you please."

"You're the trail boss, Ed," Jessie said. "How far are we from the draw now?"

"Only a couple of miles. There's a slope ahead running down to it, that's why you can't see it from here. I've passed the word to the boys to push the steers a mite faster, once they get over the hump and start down the slope. I wanted you and Ki to be ready to speed up the remuda when we start moving faster."

"We'll be ready, Ed," Jessie told him. "I'll circle the horses and tell Ki."

Jessie and Ki were still riding together when the herd began to move faster. Looking down the long slope beyond the cattle, they could see the ragged line of brush that marked the edge of Running Water Draw. The last rays of the setting sun had left the water's surface now, as the quick, short twilight of the prairie began. Already the evening shadows were showing as a dark line along the crest of the low ridge on the opposite side of the long, shallow vale in which the draw lay.

"I'd better hurry back to the other flank," Jessie said to Ki. "The steers already smell the water, and the horses will be smelling it in a few minutes. If we don't hold them back, they'll start speeding up and overrun the herd."

Spurring her mustang to a gallop, Jessie circled behind

the remuda and was in position at its flank by the time the animals smelled the water and began moving faster. She and Ki started riding in a series of tight figure-eights in front of the horses, holding them back. When they hit the downslope, the steers sped up and headed for the water, blatting eagerly, their horns tossing in shining arcs amid a sea of humping backs.

In front of them the point men rode back and forth, holding back their rush. The flankers kept in constant motion, pushing the cattle together from each side, keeping the herd from spreading and scattering. In the thick dust cloud at the rear, the drag men were kept busy chousing stragglers up to the herd. The lead steers were within a hundred yards of the water when the first shots rang out from the bushes lining the far side of the draw.

Riding behind the herd, enveloped in the cloud of dust it raised, Jessie and Ki could not at first be certain they were hearing rifle fire. They wheeled their horses and gazed toward the draw, trying to see through the dust cloud. Jessie kicked her horse into a gallop and joined Ki.

"An ambush!" she called to him as she got closer.

"Rader got here ahead of us again!" Ki shouted in reply.

Jessie gazed across the draw, and instantly her eyes were flooded with tears as she squinted into the sun. Its bright rim had not quite dropped behind the rise on the far side of the water, and with the light in her eyes and a curtain of dust hanging between her and the draw, she could not be quite sure of what she saw until her eyes adjusted to the sunlight that had blinded her momentarily.

What Jessie saw then was a scene of wild confusion. At two or three places in the front ranks of the herd, the cattle were knotting up and beginning to mill around steers that had fallen, victims of the first volley fired from the ambush.

Ed Wright and the two point men were spurring in front of the herd. They were galloping toward the water, yanking rifles from their saddle scabbards. One of the flankers on the near side was hurrying to join them. Within seconds they began shooting into the brush on the far side of the

146

draw, and as the volume of their fire increased, the ambushers broke out of the bushes and began running up the far slope.

There were only a half-dozen of them, dark figures that she could not see clearly with the sunlight on her face and the dust cloud thickening as the herd began scattering. Now and then one of the fleeing figures turned to fire, an unaimed shot that found no target.

Jessie could not tell whether the ambushers were shooting at Wright and the two point men, or just loosing bullets in the general direction of the herd. Another of the flankers on the near side broke away and galloped toward Wright and the men following him. The fleeing ambushers turned now and then to fire at the riders, ineffective snapshots that found no targets.

"Indians!" she called to Ki.

"Apaches, by the look of them," Ki responded. "Jessie, stay here and keep the remuda from breaking up! I'm going to help Wright and the men!"

"Let the remuda look out for itself!" Jessie replied. "I'm going with you!"

Slanting their horses to miss the corner of the cattle herd, Jessie and Ki streaked toward the action. Wright and the riders with him had reached the edge of the draw now, and as the horses entered the water, their progress slowed. With their eyes below the level of the brush that grew thickly along both sides of the draw, the men in the water did not see the mounted man who burst from an unusually high clump of brush and galloped after the fleeing Indians. Jessie and Ki had not yet reached the draw; their horses were still a dozen yards upslope from the bushes that lined the water's edge.

They saw the rider at almost the same instant. Ki's voice echoed Jessie's as each of them shouted, "Rader!"

Both of them were carrying their rifles. They raised their guns, but before they could get the fleeing cartel agent in their sights, the momentum of their mounts had carried them into the thick bushes.

Yanking at their reins, they turned the horses at once and spurred out of the brush. By the time they'd reached a spot where they could get a clear line of sight above the undergrowth, Rader was halfway up the slope across the draw. He was leaning forward in his saddle, his chest pressed close to the neck of his galloping horse.

Jessie and Ki leveled their rifles at the fleeing Rader, but the vees of their rear sights were fuzzy to their eyes in the fast-fading light. Both of them fired at once, but the hammer of Jessie's weapon clicked on a dead shell. By the time she'd levered a fresh load into the chamber, Ki had gotten off another shot. Rader's horse lurched and broke stride, but did not fall. Jessie lowered the muzzle of her rifle.

"No use wasting lead on him in this light!" she called to Ki. "Let's try to catch him!"

Rader had disappeared over the rim of the shallow valley, and Wright and the other hands who'd pursued the ambushers were out of the water and halfway up the slope when Jessie and Ki broke out of the brush. They shouted to the hands as they spurred their mounts in the direction Rader had been galloping, but the distance was too great for the men to hear their calls. When they reached the crest of the rise, Rader had vanished in the gloom. So had the half-dozen Apaches who'd bolted from the bushes earlier.

"We've missed him again," Ki said disgustedly.

"It looks that way," Jessie agreed reluctantly. "He can't have gotten very far, but with the light gone, there's not much chance that we'd be able to find him."

"No." Ki peered through the blue twilight at Wright and his men. "Ed's turning back. I suppose we might as well give up too. We're going to have our hands full, getting the herd and the remuda in shape."

"There's only one good thing I can see that's come from this attack," Jessie said as they turned their horses and started back toward the draw. "At least we'll be on our guard from now on, to be sure we're not caught napping again. If Rader surprises us again, it'll be our own fault."

Chapter 14

"We're just about in spitting distance of Dodge now," Ed Wright said, riding up to Jessie and reining in his horse to ride beside her. "I'd say we've put the worst behind us."

Since the unsuccessful attack at Running Water Draw, the drive had been smooth and uneventful. From the draw the herd had moved almost due north, spending only one waterless night before getting to the South Fork of the Red River at noon the next day. They'd crossed the fork and followed one of its shallow, unnamed feeder creeks for two days to within a short day's drive of the Red River's Prairie Dog Fork.

When they'd crossed the Prairie Dog Fork and were on Goodnight range, they'd had a rough day's driving over the crevassed country that lay to the north. The next day, picking up Prairie Dog Creek, the herd had eased along beside it through Palo Duro Canyon. Progress was slow along the canyon's wide, uneven floor.

Jessie reflected that only a few years earlier, a drive through Palo Duro Canyon would have been foolhardy if not suicidal. The canyon, with its high, sheltering walls and readily available water, had been the winter campgrounds of several bands of Comanches. At this time of year, in those former times, the bands would already be gathering here. Now, of course, there were very few Comanches left, in Palo Duro Canyon or anywhere else; the U. S. Army and the Texas Rangers had seen to that in a campaign more ruthless than anything the Comanches, as bloodthirsty as they were, could ever have imagined.

Emerging from the canyon at last, they came out onto unbroken, rolling prairie, over which they were now making steady progress.

Wright made no effort to keep relief from stealing into his voice as he went on, "We're so near Tascosa now that we won't make a watering stop at the head of the creek. If we just push on, we oughta make it to the Canadian by sundown."

"Yes, I looked at my map before we started this morning, and I didn't see much ahead that could slow us down, Ed," Jessie said. "Though I've heard stories about the Canadian River having a lot of quicksand holes."

"I've heard the stories too, but I've got an idea about how to beat the quicksand. It'll still be early when we hit the Canadian, and we won't be more'n a half-hour's ride from Tascosa. Maybe we can find a hand there that knows the country better than any of us do. We could hire him on for a few days, just long enough to guide us upriver someplace to where we can cross the Canadian without any trouble."

"I think it's a good idea," Jessie agreed. "Let's plan on doing that. Do you intend to lay over when we get to the river, and give the men another day off, to go into Tascosa?"

Wright rubbed the stubble on his chin. "I've been studyin' on it. They had their last time off just a little more'n a week ago, but some of 'em's been hinting about getting a chance to see Tascosa."

"It has a reputation for being a pretty rough town, Ed."

"Oh, I know that. But I've heard it's tamed down a lot, now that Billy the Kid has moved his gang over to New Mexico."

"If you think the men need another trip to town, I'd say to give it to them. What about Gimpy, though?"

"He's got supplies enough to see us through to Dodge. I'll keep him in camp, but let the men go in like they did before, half at a time, for a few hours. They'll work better for it."

"I'm sure you're right, Ed. Not that there's anything wrong with the way they've been working."

"They're a good bunch, Jessie. That Rader was the one bad apple we had. Will you and Ki be going in too?"

"As long as we're going to stop long enough for the men to blow off steam, I suppose we will."

"Then I'll set one of the boys to keep an eye on the remuda. If nobody gets in trouble in Tascosa, we won't lose much time. I'll guarantee we'll be on the move again a little after sunrise."

"For all that I've heard about it, Tascosa doesn't seem to be anything special, Jessie," Ki remarked as they looked across the Canadian River at Tascosa.

In the light of the full moon, which seemed to shine almost as brightly as the sun in the cloudless sky, they could see the town quite clearly. They'd found the crossing easily enough, though they'd started from the trail camp after sunset. The converging wheel ruts, worn deep into the flat prairie, had joined into a deep-cut set of tracks that guided them to the crossing. Where Jessie and Ki had reined in, a narrow sandspit broke water in the center of the stream. On the spit, maturing cottonwoods grew between the stumps of what had once been old trees.

Tascosa's main street lay only two lariat-lengths from the opposite bank, and between the thin boles and high-growing, broad-leaved branches of the saplings, they could see houses straggling along the wide yellow streak of the street. After splashing across the river, Jessie and Ki rode slowly along the sandy road, taking stock of the little community as their horses ambled ahead.

For the most part, Tascosa was a tan town. Even by moonlight, Jessie and Ki could see the earthy hues of adobe

151

and cut sandstone that predominated in the walls of the houses as well as the business buildings. One notable exception was a sprawling store building faced with white-painted, pressed-tin panels that shone like silver in the bright moonlight. It was twice as big as any of the other stores, and dominated a corner near the center of the settlement. The sign over the sidewalk awning read *Howard & McMasters, General Merchandise*.

They rode on, past the smaller stores and the light-spilling batwings of the saloons, to the point where they could see that the houses ahead were huddled close together as though for mutual protection, and were marked by red lanterns hanging over their doors. Jessie reined in.

"I suppose we'd better turn back, Ki," she said. "If I know cowhands, they'll be heading this way as soon as they've had a few drinks. I'm sure they'd feel funny if they ran into us on the street."

"That's something I've never understood about this country," Ki commented as they turned their horses and started back to the center of town. "The mutual pretense game that men and women play of ignoring sex publicly and enjoying it privately."

"Well, privacy has some points in its favor," Jessie said. "But I suppose someday we'll accept sex as a fact of life, just as people do in Europe and Asia."

They reached the center of town, and Jessie pulled her horse over to the hitch rail in front of the Howard & McMasters store.

"I didn't know this was going to be a shopping trip," Ki said, then followed Jessie's example as she dismounted and looped the reins over the rail.

"Have you forgotten the dud shell I had in my rifle back at Running Water Draw? It spoiled the only chance I had for a shot at Rader. I want to buy a box of fresh shells, but my main reason for stopping here is to exchange one of my hundred-dollar gold certificates for coins."

When the clerk laid on the counter the box of shells

Jessie asked for, she turned her back long enough to un-button her blouse and reach into the money belt in which she carried the money for supplies and other trail expenses. Slipping out one of the hundred-dollar gold certificates from the compartment in which she carried the large-denomination currency, she rebuttoned her shirt, turned back to the counter, and offered the crisp, yellow-backed certificate to the clerk.

"Oh, my," he said. "Don't you have anything smaller, ma'am? The shells are only a dollar and fifteen cents a box."

"Unless you're short of cash, I'd really appreciate it if you'd change the bill for me," Jessie said. "I've got a trail herd just outside town, on the way to Dodge City, and except for some small change, all I have is these gold certificates."

"It's not that we're short of cash," the clerk explained. "But except for change money, it's locked up in the safe, and Mr. Howard's out of town and Mr. McMasters has gone home for the day. I'll be glad to change the bill for you, ma'am if you don't mind taking half of it in cartwheels."

"I don't mind in the least," Jessie replied.

She watched as the clerk opened the till and took out an eagle and two double eagles, laid them on the counter, then began piling silver dollars in neat stacks of ten. When he had five stacks of ten dollars each, he took two of the silver coins off one of the piles and dropped them back in the till, placed a half-dollar, a twenty-five-cent piece, and a dime beside the stack he'd shorted, and waved at the array.

"I think that's right, ma'am," he said. "And thank you for your custom."

"It's a pleasure," Jessie replied. She waited until the clerk moved down the counter to attend to another customer, then dropped the coins into her money belt and buttoned her blouse. She said to Ki, "Unless you have something else in mind, Ki, I've taken care of all the business I had in Tascosa."

"Back to camp, then," Ki said. "We've seen the town,

and we certainly don't have any reason for staying here."

As they stepped out onto the board sidewalk, they saw Ed Wright and a stranger crossing the street, heading for the store. Wright called to them, and they waited until he and the other man reached the walk.

"You remember the talk we had about hiring on a hand who knows the Canadian crossings, Jessie?" Wright said. When Jessie nodded, he went on, "I think I've found the man we need. This is Cal Snider. Cal, this is my boss I was telling you about, Miss Jessie Starbuck, who owns the Circle Star."

Snider doffed his wide-brimmed hat as Jessie extended her hand. He said, "Mr. Wright says you're a good boss, Miss Starbuck. I'll try to be a good hand for you."

"I'm sure you will," Jessie told him. "Ed's told you the job's temporary, hasn't he?"

"Yes, ma'am, that suits me fine. I was aiming to head up the same way you are, to see if there's any jobs going up in that part of the Panhandle."

Jessie was evaluating Snider as he spoke. He was a young man who somehow looked old. Jessie decided this was because of a scar that ran from the outer corner of his left eye in a long weal that ended at the corner of his mouth and pulled his lips into a permanent twist. He needed a shave, and his clothing was stained and dust-covered, but Jessie did not count the scar, his unshaven cheeks, or the condition of his clothes against him; these were commonplace on any ranch.

She said, "I'm sure you've worked around here long enough to learn the river, or Ed wouldn't have hired you."

"Oh, I know the Canadian, Miss Starbuck," Snider assured her. "Not just the main branch, but the North Canadian too. You'll have to cross it up in No Man's Land, you know."

"Does it have quicksand pockets like the main river?" Jessie asked.

"It ain't as bad, but you got to know where to hit it,"

Snider replied. "I can show you where. I've handed and drove for the Cator brothers up on the Diamond C, and Berry and Boyce on the Sevens spread, east of the Cators', and Tom Bugbee down south of 'em, on the Quarter-Circle T."

"Well, we'll be glad to have you," Jessie said. She turned to Wright. "Are you going back to the herd now? If you are, we can ride together."

"Thanks, Jessie, but I'll be drifting around town, seeing that the boys all stay out of trouble and start for camp in time to get some shut-eye before we head out in the morning. I aim to be the last one to leave, after I'm sure they're all headed back."

"Then we'd better start back, Ki, before Ed shoos us out of town," Jessie smiled. "I'd hate to be blamed for getting us off to a late start in the morning."

"I don't see how we've done it, either," Ki said, looking at the position of Jessie's finger on the map she'd spread over the rump of her pony. "Of course, Rader hasn't tried any new tricks since we left Running Water Draw, and that's helped."

"I can't believe he's given up," Jessie said. "I've told Ed to keep a close lookout. The cartel never quits, Ki, we both know that."

They were standing in front of the remuda on the north bank of Palo Duro Creek, only a few miles now from the northern border of Texas, waiting for the herd to get a good start before putting the horses into motion. It was a clear, bright morning which promised that the day would be as pleasant as those they'd had since starting along the Canadian River from Tascosa.

Jessie went on, "I'm sure one reason we've made such good time is that we've had a good trail to follow. Why, Gimpy's been able to ride with the herd, because all he's had to do is look for the coals left by the last herd to find the best place to pull up the chuckwagon."

"That new man, Cal Snider, he's helped too," Ki said. "He knows where to drive around the rough places instead of wasting time trying to go straight across them."

"Yes," Jessie agreed. "And he saved us the better part of a day by showing us exactly where to cross the Canadian."

"I'm sure we've covered more ground in the five days since we left Tascosa than we usually cover in a week," Ki said. "And some of it's been pretty tough going over bad country."

"Let's just be glad we have a good guide, Ki. If what Snider's told Ed is right, we have only one more bad river ahead, that's the North Fork of the Canadian."

"How about the Arkansas at Dodge City?" Ki asked.

Jessie shook her head. "Ed says the crossing there is used all the time. We shouldn't have any trouble on the Arkansas." She looked at the herd and added, "We'd better get the remuda moving, Ki. There's enough distance between us and the herd now so that we won't have to eat too much dust."

Steadily the herd plodded on across the prairie while the sun crossed the sky. During the waning hours of the afternoon, at some point a few miles after they'd forded Palo Duro Creek, the steers finally moved out of Texas. No one was exactly sure where or when they crossed the Texas border and entered what Snider had told them at supper the night before was called No Man's Land.

This was a strip of territory not quite forty miles wide and a bit more than a hundred fifty miles long that had been created by the surveyors marking the boundaries between Texas, Kansas, and the Indian Nation. Working independently of each other, the two crews had gotten the Cimarron and Canadian Rivers mixed up—not hard to do, since the courses of the two rivers run roughly parallel.

One surveying party, working southward along the western boundary between Kansas and Colorado, had started east from the Cimarron to mark the southern border of Kansas. The second surveying party, working northward in

Texas along its border with New Mexico, had mistaken the Canadian for the Cimarron and turned east at that river. Neither of the surveying parties realized until two or three years later that each of them had mistakenly stopped at the wrong river.

By then, settlers had found that except for a narrow band a mile or so on each side of the sinuous North Fork of the Canadian River, the land in the strip that the error had created was barren and waterless. Prospective farmers and ranchers moved on to better land, where water and graze were more plentiful, and more importantly, to a place where they could get a clear title to whatever land they home-steaded.

Both Texas and Kansas refused to claim the long, narrow rectangle, while the administrators in Washington kept in-sisting that it was not federal property. As a result, the wanted and the hunted of the adjoining states, as well as renegades from the tribes that had been resettled in the Indian Nation, used it as a refuge where there was no law except that of the gun and blade.

"But I don't look for us to have any trouble," Snider had assured them. "Anybody that's in No Man's Land sure ain't there because they wanta be, and they got all the trouble they can handle, or they wouldn't be there in the first place."

Snider had been given one of the point positions when the herd started along the Canadian, so that he could be close to Wright, whose job it was to guide the herd. When he saw the river a half-mile in front of the herd, Wright spurred back to find the new hand.

"What river is that one just ahead?" he called. "Am I right in taking it for the North Fork of the Canadian?"

Standing up in his stirrups, Snider looked ahead. "That's what it is, all right," he called back. "Wheel the steers a mite to the east and we'll hit the crossing right on the button."

"You sure about that?" Wright asked. "It looks to me like the drive-trail goes right on ahead to the river."

"It used to, until a couple of years ago, when the bank got undercut during a flood," Snider replied. "The new trail ain't been used enough yet to be plain."

"Funny," Wright said with a frown, "I didn't see any sign of the bank being undercut."

"You don't notice it until you're right at the river," Snider told him. "But this old crossing has sure turned into a bad one."

"Go ahead and start swinging, then," Wright told him. "Let's don't wait till we get crowded against the riverbank. I'll catch Strawfoot's eye and have him swing wide."

When the herd had to be turned quickly in a short radius, it was the job of the point men to pivot the lead steers. Strawfoot was the pivot-man this time. He saw Wright's hand signal and started veering off at right angles to the new direction, while at the opposite point Snider began crowding the lead steers into a new course at a forty-five-degree angle to the direction in which they'd been plodding. The flankers saw the change and shifted their courses, taking their cues from the moves of the point men in front of them.

In the same way that a caterpillar will swing its head suddenly in a new direction and its body will turn at the point where the head shifted, the herd was soon moving east along the Canadian's North Fork. Riding with the remuda, Jessie and Ki saw the change of direction almost at once, and followed the herd in its new course beside the river, but still a half-mile from its bank.

After the herd had traveled more than two miles and the sun had dropped almost to the horizon behind the plodding steers, Wright began to get edgy. He rode back to Snider's point.

"When do we hit that new crossing?" he asked. "I want to get the critters across before dark, if we can."

"Pretty soon now," Snider replied. "Not more'n another half-mile or so. I'll give you a wave when we get to the place."

Nodding, the Circle Star foreman rode back to his lead

spot in front of the steers. They'd forged ahead another half-mile when Wright, taking one of his frequent looks back at Snider to be sure he'd get the signal at once, saw the new hand waving and gesturing to indicate that they'd reached the spot to turn toward the river. Wright relayed the signal to Strawfoot, and in a moment the herd was beginning to change its direction, heading once more for the river.

Wright let the herd catch up with him now. He held his pony in, moving almost as slowly as the cattle, studying the terrain, his mind on the now-familiar moves that would be necessary within the next few minutes to begin squeezing the steers into the narrow column for the river crossing.

He was within fifty yards of the stream when he suddenly realized that something was wrong. The ground ahead bore no prints of cattle hooves. If a herd had crossed at this point at any time in the recent past, it had left no sign of its passing. Reining in, Wright studied the ground a moment longer to be sure his eyes weren't deceiving him.

He was reaching for his reins to turn his horse and gallop back as quickly as possible to stop the herd when he heard a faint scuffing on the ground behind him. Before he could turn to look, a gruff voice spoke.

"You not move! Put hands up, fast!"

Chapter 15

There was no mistaking the menace in the voice. Wright raised his hands above his head. Feet scuffled on the hard-baked crusty soil behind him. Four men moved around Wright's horse, keeping their distance. Wright stared at them, his jaw set and his lips pressed into a thin angry line as they stopped a half-dozen feet from him, two on either side.

As they moved into position, Wright flicked his eyes over them, quick glances from one to another, taking stock quickly as they stared at him with deep-set obsidian eyes. All four of the men wore covert-cloth jeans with loose shirts tucked into them, and all but one were shod in moccasins, the fourth in battered boots. Their skins were dark, and they had the square-jawed, flattened faces that marked them either as Comanches or Kiowas, though one of them looked as though he might be a half-breed. All four had weapons ready in their hands. Two carried rifles, one a pistol, and one a sawed-off, double-barreled shotgun.

"What've you got on your mind?" Wright asked, turning his head from one pair to the other, trying to pick out the leader.

"Money," grunted the man holding the pistol.

"A holdup?" Wright smiled at the man thinly. "Hell, I ain't got enough cash in my jeans to buy you a bottle of whiskey, if that's what you're after."

"Not whiskey. Not holdup," the leader said. "You pay us to cross river."

"In a pig's eye, I will!" Wright snorted. "This ain't your river. It runs through public land. Anybody can cross it without paying you a penny!"

"This No Man's Land!" the leader replied calmly. "River belongs to anybody claims it. We claim it, so is ours. You want to cross cattle, you pay."

"Damn it, you can't lay claim to a river!" Wright exclaimed angrily. "Rivers belong to everybody, always have!"

"Not here. Rivers belong to whoever got guns. You pay!"

Wright shook his head. "Not a penny. We'll move downriver, find another place to cross."

"You not move cattle," the leader said. "You try, we shoot you, we shoot men, we shoot steers."

"Them steers belong to the Circle Star and Box B ranches down in South Texas!"

"This not South Texas. This No Man's Land," the man said calmly. "We claim river, we claim land. You got steers on our land, they got no right there, so we shoot if you don't pay!"

Wright placed the men at once as renegades, and saw at the same time the seriousness of the man's threat. He had a mental picture of the havoc that would follow if the four men began firing into the herd. The smell of blood would send the cattle into a panicked stampede, and the herd would scatter in the darkness beyond hope of being gathered again.

Already the light was fading fast. The full moon had begun to glow a bright silver in the eastern sky, and the last rays of the setting sun bathed the western heavens in gold. Wright decided the situation was one that he could not handle alone. He was ready to call for help, but he wanted to send Jessie as much information as he could.

"How much do you want to let the herd across?" he asked.

"Two American dollar a head," the leader answered calmly.

"Two dol—" Wright shouted before he regained control. He stopped and held his anger in check until he could speak calmly. "You know how many steers is in that herd?"

"Sure. We watch all day. Big herd, mebbe two thousan'."

"Them steers ain't mine," Wright said. "So I can't promise to pay you a penny. I just work for the lady that owns most of 'em. You'll have to talk to her."

"Get lady. We tell her." The leader nodded.

"How do you expect me to go get her, with you holding your guns on me?"

"Turn horse slow," the leader said. "You go, we go. You call one man, send him get lady."

Before he lowered his hands to the reins, Wright said, "It might help if I can tell the lady who she's got to talk to. Mind telling me your names?"

"What names mean?" the man asked. He spat expressively, then the corners of his mouth turned down and he said, "Tell her me, Hainenri."

"Kiowa?"

"Comanche. Now, turn horse! Not waste time!"

Wright turned his horse. He was surprised that his captors had made no move to take his rifle and pistol, but when he'd wheeled the pony around, he understood why they hadn't thought it necessary. Two more men stood behind him, shotguns leveled. As he toed the pony ahead, Hainenri and one of the other men who'd been in front of him closed in and walked beside him.

They'd covered only half the distance to the herd, which was still turning toward the river, when Wright saw the new hand, Cal Snider, riding toward them. Before Wright could raise his voice, Hainenri said, "Man come now. Send him get lady."

Though Wright would have preferred to see Will Grant or one of the regular hands, he had no choice. Before Snider got too close, he called, "Snider! Pull up right where you are!" When the new man reined in, Wright went on, "I want you to go back to the remuda and get Miss Starbuck and

163

Ki! Tell 'em these men want to be paid to let the herd cross the river!"

"Paid?" Snider asked.

"That's right. Two dollars a head. They say if they don't get it, they'll start shooting into the herd."

"Hell, them fellows look like they'd do it, too!" Snider said as he reined in. "You sure you don't need some help besides Miss Starbuck and her man, Ed?"

"I'm all right. Just tell Jessie what's happening and tell her I need both her and Ki to get up here in a hurry!"

"Sure. I'm on my way."

Jessie and Ki had halted the remuda fifty yards or so behind the herd and were waiting for the steers to begin crossing the North Canadian. As the sunlight faded and darkness began to settle in, Ki rode around the horse herd to the opposite side, where Jessie was stationed.

"I can't think of anything that would hold Ed up as long as this," he said. "Do you think there's something wrong?"

"You know how careful Ed is," she reminded him. "More than likely he's just checking the crossing himself, to make sure it's all right before he starts the herd across."

"If the cattle don't start moving soon, it'll be the middle of the night before they're all on the other side, Jessie."

"As late as we are getting the crossing started, I wouldn't be surprised if we stayed on this side tonight and waited for daylight to cross."

"I'm not sure about that," Ki said. "If we were going to stay here tonight, Ed would've had Gimpy start supper by now. I can see the chuckwagon from the other side of the remuda, and Gimpy's still just sitting in it, waiting."

"Well, whatever Ed decides will be fine with me," Jessie said. "Still, you'd think—" she broke off and pointed to Cal Snider, who was riding across the space between the herd and the remuda. "It looks like we're about to find out what's happening. I imagine Snider's bringing word from Ed."

164

Snider reined in as he reached Jessie and Ki, and said, "Mr. Wright wants you to ride up to the head of the herd, Ki. He's got something he'd like to talk to you about."

"Do you know what he wants to talk about?" Ki asked.

"I sure don't. He just told me he'd like for you to ride up to where he is."

Ki turned to Jessie. "Perhaps we'd both better go," he said.

Jessie shook her head. "No, Ki. If Ed had wanted me to go, he'd have said so." She looked at Snider. "Is anything wrong at the river? Someone hurt, something like that?"

"No ma'am," Snider replied. "There's just a bunch of fellows looks like Indians that Mr. Wright's having a palaver with."

"Indians?" Ki asked.

"That's what they look like to me," Snider answered.

"If it's Indians, they may be begging for a steer or two. I understand government rations on their reservations leave a lot to be desired," Jessie said thoughtfully. "And you know how Indians feel about women mixing into men's business, Ki. That's probably why Ed asked for you to come up instead of me."

"I'll go on, then," Ki said. He nudged the ribs of his pony with his boot toe. "Are you coming, Snider?"

"Sure. I'll be right behind you."

Ki slapped the reins of his mount and started away. Jessie watched him for a moment, and when the new hand made no move to follow him, she turned around to ask why he hadn't gone with Ki. She found herself looking into the muzzle of Snider's revolver.

"Just set right still, Miss Starbuck," Snider said. His voice was as cold as chilled steel, and the long, slanting scar on his cheek was glowing rosy red. "I'd hate to have to kill a pretty woman like you, but I sure as hell will if you try to get away."

Her voice sharp, Jessie said, "Don't be a fool, Snider! Put that gun away!"

"You ain't giving orders here now, *Miss* Starbuck," he replied. "And I ain't got time to waste jawing with you. Now you do what I tell you to, or I'll kill you."

Jessie had no doubt that he was ready to carry out his threat. She said, "All right. What is it you want me to do?"

"Rein your horse around, but don't try to kick it up. Just stay still." When Jessie had turned her horse, she heard the slow clopping of the hooves of Snider's mount as he came up behind her. He leaned from the saddle and slid her Colt from its holster. "I'll have to leave your rifle where it's at, for now," he said. "But I'll be riding right in back of you with my gun in my hand, and if you make a move to get it, you're dead. You got that?"

Thinking of the derringer she had concealed in her boot, Jessie pretended to be alarmed. Forcing into her voice a fear she did not feel, she said meekly, "Yes. I understand."

"Now start riding back the way we just come. Don't yell or do nothing foolish and you're likely to live a while longer."

Again Jessie obeyed. She followed the hoofprints the herd had made as it was being driven to the river. She did not need to look back to make sure Snider was directly behind her; she could tell that from the sound of his horse's hooves.

As they rode, the last rays of the sun faded from the western sky, and the darkness deepened quickly. Jessie knew that in a very few minutes they would be too far from the herd for the men to see them. She decided the only way that she could escape would be to wait until the night blackened further and then kick her horse into a quick leap and gallop off while she bent over its neck to make the smallest possible target. Even then, she judged her chance to be less than fifty-fifty. With Snider so close, his gun ready in his hand, it would be almost impossible for him to miss. Then he ordered her to rein in, and even that faint hope vanished.

"Pull up now," Snider said. "We're far enough away so they can't see us from the herd, and I don't trust you one damn inch." He pulled his horse up beside Jessie's and fished a pigging string from the pocket of his jeans. "Put your hands down on your saddlehorn," he went on. "I ain't taking no chances. If you was to try to bolt, you just might make it. I'll be leading your horse the rest of the way."

Leaning from his saddle, Snider began tying Jessie's wrists to the saddlehorn with quick, dexterous twists. He tied off the narrow leather thong with the quickly formed knot that he must have used many times in securing the hooves of bulldogged steers. While he worked, Jessie kept her forearm muscles tensed and spread her fingers wide to enlarge her wrists, but Snider showed no mercy. When he pulled the leather thong tight, it cut into her wrists cruelly.

"Well now," he said when he'd finished. "That oughta hold you, but I'll just take your rifle, in case you're smart enough to get your hands loose." He lifted the rifle from its saddle scabbard and went on, "Now, then, we'll be moving again. Likely you got a good deal of money in your saddlebags, but I reckon it's safe enough to let you carry it till I'm ready to take it."

Lifting the reins of Jessie's pony, Snider tied them to one of his saddlestrings and secured the rifle to another. He toed his horse ahead, leading Jessie's horse now, and they moved slowly off into the yawning blackness that gaped beyond the edge of the moonlight.

Jessie wasted no time. As soon as Snider's back was turned she began spreading her elbows, holding them away from her body, working them back and forth to create slack in the leather thong binding her wrists. She had no illusions about the fate that was waiting for her. By now she was certain that Snider had been hired by Rader, and that the cartel's merciless operative would be waiting, wherever Snider might take her.

Snider's remark about money had given her an idea. She knew that as soon as Ki missed her, he'd begin trying to pick up their trail and follow them. She also realized that even Ki's keen eyes could not see hoofprints on the hard prairie soil in the darkness. The success of her half-formed plan depended on her being able to leave a trail he could pick up. Forcing herself to be patient, she kept her elbows moving steadily, forward and back, while Snider led her farther and farther from the herd.

When Ki responded to Snider's faked message from Wright, he rode off at a gallop. He did not look back at once to be sure the new hand was following him, and when he did, he'd already gone past the rear of the herd. He saw that Snider was not behind him, but decided that the restlessly milling steers hid him in the growing darkness. He kept going until he reached the front corner of the herd.

Looking back again, still seeing no sign that Snider was behind him, Ki frowned. His intuition told him that something was wrong. For a moment he debated turning back, but remembering the many times when Jessie had proved her ability to take care of herself in an emergency, he decided that Wright's message must be his first concern. He reined his horse to a walk and continued riding toward the bank of the river.

While he was still twenty yards or more from the stream, Ki could see Wright and the Comanches silhouetted against the moon-silvered surface of the river. He was close enough now to see the muzzles of the rifles and shotguns held by the Indians. Ki studied their positions carefully while he covered the remaining distance.

As he rode, Ki slipped four star-shaped *shuriken* from one of the many pockets of his leather vest and put them in his left hand, holding the reins with his right. When he'd closed the remaining distance and was within a dozen feet of the group, Ki pulled up his horse. The renegades reacted as he'd expected them to. They turned their full attention away from Wright and shifted their positions slightly to cover Ki with their weapons. Ki saw at a glance that their most formidable weapons were the three shotguns, and paid special but casual attention to the men holding them.

Keeping his voice low, acting puzzled, Ki scanned the

group of Comanches before he asked, "What's your trouble up here, Ed?"

Hainenri did not give Wright a chance to reply. He broke in suspiciously, saying, "You not lady. Where she?"

"She sent me in her place, to find out what's wrong," Ki replied calmly. When Hainenri still glared at him with open suspicion, Ki raised his hands above his head. "Look. I have no pistol, I came only to talk." As Ki had planned, his gesture and words drew the attention of the Comanches to his waist, and while he held his hands high, he slid two of the *shuriken* disks into his right hand. Lowering his arms slowly, Ki asked, "Who are you?"

"Hainenri. You bring American dollars?"

Wright broke in before Ki could reply. He said, "You know I didn't tell the man I sent to have anybody bring money back here, Hainenri. You heard what I told him."

"I heard," Hainenri replied, his broad face wrinkling into a frown as he recalled the message Wright had told Snider to deliver. He turned back to Ki and said, "You go get money now!"

"Of course I won't," Ki said quietly. "Why should I?"

"You don't pay us two dollar every steer, you not cross river, we shoot cattle," Hainenri answered. He jerked his head to indicate Wright. "Man he send to get lady know that."

Ki stalled purposely. His years of martial-arts training had impressed on him that the success of his tactics in a situation like this one depended on studying the enemy as carefully as possible while distracting him with casual conversation and trying to lull him into a sense of false security before making a hostile move.

"That's a lot of money you want, Hainenri," Ki said. "How do we know you'll leave us alone if we give it to you?"

"You pay, we go," Hainenri grunted impatiently. "Now you go get lady, tell her bring money fast!"

Ki realized that his time for stalling had run out, but he'd achieved his purpose. He raised his head, looking along the riverbank beyond the Indians. They reacted as he'd expected, their eyes followed his.

"Fall, Ed!" Ki snapped.

He could not wait to see whether Wright obeyed, for at the sound of his voice the Comanches turned their attention back to him. Ki had slipped one of the two *shuriken* in each of his hands into throwing position. As this forced him to hold the other two blades in his palms, he could not launch the wicked, razor-edged throwing stars with his customary forceful snap, but had to flick them with a short backhand motion of his wrists.

His aim remained true, though. The razor-sharp *shuriken* flicked with Ki's right hand sailed the short distance to Hainenri's face. One of the points penetrated the renegade's eyeball, sending out a spurt of vitreous matter and blinding the leader of the band.

Ki's second *shuriken* sped from his left hand and sliced into the cheek of one of the men holding a shotgun. The Comanche was bringing up his weapon to fire, but the shock of the *shuriken* ripping into his face made him trigger the weapon while its muzzle was still pointed downward. The recoil tore the loosely held gun from the man's hands and it dropped to the ground while he clawed at his face, trying to remove the blade.

Ed Wright had rolled out of his saddle when he heard Ki's warning shout. He drew his Colt as he hit the ground, and let off two quick shots at the man standing nearest him. It was one of the Comanches who carried a shotgun, and Wright's slugs knocked him down before he could bring up the weapon. Rising to his knees, the foreman looked quickly for another target.

Ki's hands were unencumbered as soon as he'd flicked the first two *shuriken*. He could get a firm throwing grip on the second pair, and sent one of them whirling to the throat of the Comanche who held the remaining shotgun. The Indian was standing several yards away, at the edge of the group, and he saw the moonlight glinting on the bright surface of the blade.

Instead of aiming the shotgun at Ki, he swiveled its muzzle to fire at the *shuriken*. The lead pellets deflected it, but Ki had followed up his throw with another immediately, and this one took the man in his throat. He stood transfixed for a second or two after the *shuriken* bit into his jugular vein, then slowly crumpled to the ground as a gush of blood spread over his blouse.

Wright had found other targets immediately after bringing down the Comanche who'd held the shotgun. Still prone, he fired between the legs of the horses at one of the remaining Indians. The slug hit the renegade low, in the groin, and he doubled up, grasping at his crotch, as the bullet plowed into him.

After throwing his last *shuriken*, Ki slid his feet from his stirrups, brought his legs up, and launched himself from the saddle at the last of the renegades. He drew his *tanto* as he sailed through the air, and as he hit the man he slid the point of the curved blade between the renegade's ribs and into his heart. The Indian gasped once in his death-throes, then lay motionless.

Ki got to his feet. The entire fight had lasted only a few seconds. Four of the six renegades were dead or dying. Hainenri was still clawing at his eyes, and the man Wright had wounded in the groin was doubled over, moaning in pain. On the other side of the horses, Wright was getting to his feet.

"Ed, I'll leave this mess for you to clean up," Ki said. "Get the boys to give you a hand. You know what to do."

"You're worried about Jessie, I guess?"

"Of course I am. I don't have any proof, but I'm very sure Rader planned this whole setup. I'm sure, now, that Snider's got to be Rader's man. He was supposed to follow me here, but he must have stayed behind and captured Jessie, or she'd be here herself by now. I've got to get to her, Ed, before Snider delivers her to Rader!"

Chapter 16

While she was struggling to free her hands from the pigging string, Jessie kept her composure. Like Ki, she had realized at once that Snider must be taking her to Rader; there could be no other reason for him to make her a prisoner.

From the moment they'd left the herd, it had been obvious to Jessie that Snider had a destination in mind. He moved ahead unhesitatingly, without stopping to study the terrain or to look at their surroundings. He stayed in the wide swath of prairie that had been broken and trampled by the herd on its way to the river. The pocked hoofmarks left by the steers showed clearly in the bright moonlight, and Jessie's heart sank when she realized that even such an expert tracker as Ki would find it impossible to pick out the hoofprints of two horses on the broken ground.

She kept her eyes on Snider's back while she continued to work at freeing her hands. He'd looked back at her at frequent intervals when they first started, but as they'd gotten farther from the herd, his over-the-shoulder glances became less frequent. She estimated they'd been riding for almost a half hour before Snider checked his horse and began looking closely at the area on the south side of the herd's trail, as though trying to find a landmark.

Jessie's unceasing efforts had created a tiny bit of slack in her bonds by then, and just before Snider began angling off the wide swath marked by the herd, she folded her thumb into the palm of her hand and, with a slow, steady pull, managed to free the hand. Loosened now, the pigging string was slack and her other hand slid out easily. She flexed her fingers until their numbness vanished and feeling returned to them. She was starting to lean down and pull the derringer from her boot when she saw Snider's shoulders begin to shift.

Jessie's quick reflexes saved her. By the time Snider had completed his turn, she was sitting erect, with her hands folded on the saddlehorn. Snider glanced at her hands, flicked his gaze up to her face, then faced forward again. Brief as the interruption of her move had been, it had given Jessie time to think and reconsider. More positive than ever that Snider was taking her to Rader, she discarded the idea of shooting him now. Jessie set her sights on bigger game, and began to carry out the plan that had occurred to her earlier.

Unbuttoning her blouse at the waist, Jessie scooped a handful of silver dollars out of the money belt and dropped one of the coins to the ground just before Snider led her horse off the hoofmarked strip. The newly minted cartwheel caught the moon's glow, and she kept her eyes on it, a tiny bright dot on the dark earth, shining like a beacon in the bright moonlight.

Counting seconds silently, Jessie watched the glow until it was almost invisible, then dropped another dollar. Knowing now how long to wait before leaving the next marker, she returned to her former position, her hands folded on the saddlehorn as though they were still tied. Counting the intervals carefully, she let one cartwheel after another slip through her fingers as they rode through the night, hoping that Snider wouldn't decide to turn and check on her just as she released one of the coins.

Snider did glance back at her several times, but did not speak. Jessie's luck was unusually good, for he never caught her actually letting one of the dollars drop, though once or twice he turned his head within a few seconds after she'd let one of the coins slide out of her hand.

They'd been riding for another half hour when Jessie saw the light ahead. It seemed to leap into her field of vision, for while it was surrounded by the stars that filled the sky's inverted bowl, the light was yellow and the stars were blue-white. The source of the light was still some distance away. Jessie let a dollar drop to the ground and held another in reserve in her palm while she returned the few that remained to the money belt and buttoned her blouse.

Gradually the square shape of a small structure took shape ahead in the darkness. The pinpoint of light grew larger and brighter. As they drew closer to it, Jessie could see that the light came from a line shack, one of the small shelters most large ranches provided along their boundaries to shelter cowhands assigned to distant grazing areas, or to be used by fence riders caught out in bad weather.

Snider looked over his shoulder at her for several seconds before they reached the shack and he reined in. Then he shifted in his saddle and turned, half-facing her.

"I guess you figured out by now what's going on," he said. "If you ain't, you're a long way from being as smart as I heard you are."

"I'm sure you've brought me to where your boss is waiting," Jessie replied. "And I'm equally sure his name—or at least the name I know him by—is Rader."

Snider chuckled. "Damned if you ain't got it taped. Looks like you're a pretty smart one after all. But not smart enough to outguess us, was you?"

Jessie did not reply, and he went on, "I guess I might as well let you get off, now that we got to where we was headed."

Jessie had not been able to figure out a way to retie her hands in the same manner that Snider had tied them. She swung out of the saddle before he could step up to her horse, and when she turned to face him after dismounting, his jaw was hanging slack in surprise.

"You're a hell of a sight smarter'n I figured!" he snapped. "Lucky I took your rifle, or I guess I'd be dead by now!"

"You certainly would have been, if I'd had a gun," Jessie said coolly. "And if I'd gotten my hands loose a few minutes sooner, you'd be looking for me out on the prairie right now!"

"Well, you didn't, and I ain't! And you'll pay for being so damn smart before the night's over!" he snarled. Grabbing Jessie's arm roughly, he led her to the source of the light, a crack in the shack's door. A step or two before he reached the door, he called softly, "Rader! It's me, and I got the woman!"

Ki spurred his horse to a gallop when he left Ed Wright at the river and returned to the remuda. As he raced past the last steers in the herd, a thought occurred to him. Reining in, he peered through the dark, looking for one of the drag men. A short distance away, Mossy sat on his horse. Ki toed his horse ahead and stopped beside Mossy.

"Have you seen Jessie?" he asked.

"Not for a while, Ki. Last time I looked around, she was by the remuda there, talkin' to the new hand, that Snider."

"You didn't see them leave?"

Mossy shook his head. "If they left, they sure didn't pass by me, or I'd of noticed 'em."

For a moment Ki debated possibilities. He'd left the remuda nearly an hour ago. Depending on how fast they'd ridden, Jessie and Snider could be anywhere from three to six miles away by now. He stared into the moonlit night, into the darkness that made tracking impossible even for his keen eyes.

Suddenly the thought came to him that if his suspicion was correct—if Snider had kidnapped Jessie to deliver her to Rader—the only way the cartel agent had of knowing the herd's position was by following it. Since Snider had joined the drive in Tascosa, Rader must have been following the herd since it left there, and he would now be stationed somewhere along the backtrail, waiting for Snider to deliver Jessie to him.

Ki realized that his logic was thin at best, but if offered the only starting point he could think of to begin his search. Turning his pony along the wide path broken by the hooves of the steers, he began riding slowly along it.

Jessie felt no fear, only anger, as she stood beside Snider in the darkness outside the line shack, waiting for Rader to open the door. The door opened, and both she and Snider blinked as the light of the lantern burning inside the shack flooded around the tall, lean, silhouetted figure of the cartel operative and struck their night-dilated eyes.

"Well, get her inside, Snider!" Rader commanded curtly. "A light can be seen for a long way on this flat prairie."

Blinking in what seemed a brilliant glare, Jessie let Snider push her through the door. Rader grabbed her hand and yanked her farther into the cabin.

"You damned fool!" he said angrily to Snider. "Why aren't her hands tied?"

"They was, until a minute ago," Snider replied. "She got 'em loose just about the time we rode up."

"Then tie them now!" Rader ordered. "There's a piece of an old lariat hanging on that nail. Use it!"

Jessie did not struggle as Snider lashed her arms again. He did not tie her wrists this time, but pulled her arms behind her back and looped the rope above her elbows, knotted it firmly, then brought the end up and tied it around her neck. Even the slightest movement of Jessie's arms pulled the neck-loop taut and started it to strangling her. When his knot was completed, Snider pushed her down into a chair.

While she was being tied, Jessie's eyes had adjusted to the lanternlight. She looked around. The little one-room building was furnished with the bare minimum required by a man or two for a short stay: one chair in addition to the one in which she was sitting, a battered kitchen table, a narrow, two-tiered bunk bed, and one of the small oblong stoves that cowhands called a "monkey stove." The lantern hung above the table, suspended at the end of a length of wire with one end bent into a hook.

"These aren't the kind of surroundings you're used to, I'm sure, Miss Starbuck," Rader said mockingly, standing in front of her. His voice was as rough as a blacksmith's file. "But we'll only be here for a few hours. At daybreak, you and I will be on our way to join my colleagues. There is a great deal we expect you to tell us about the operations of various Starbuck enterprises."

"To help you loot them or wreck them, I'm sure," Jessie said calmly. "You know I won't tell you anything, Rader."

"I'm afraid you haven't learned much from the lessons I've given you during your cattle drive," the cartel man said. "Each time, I've outwitted you. No, you're not as clever as you think you are."

"We've gotten the cattle this far in spite of what you call your lessons, Rader," Jessie retorted. "They haven't been very clever either, have they?"

Rader's thin lips split in an unpleasant grimace that was intended to be a smile. "The lessons waiting for you will be more forceful. Our persuasions will be uncomfortable, some of them quite painful, but we know there are limits to the amount of pain anyone can stand. Even you have limits."

While Jessie and Rader talked, Snider had been poking around in the corners of the little cabin. He came and stood beside Rader now and asked, "What time we pulling out in the morning?"

"I'll be leaving with the Starbuck woman as soon as there's enough light to travel by," Rader replied. "You'll be leaving as soon as you can get on your horse and ride off."

"Wait a minute now!" Snider protested. The scar on his face began to flush redly. "You promised me this was just going to be the first one of a lot of jobs you'd have for me!"

Rader dug a handful of mixed gold and silver coins from his pocket. He began stacking gold eagles on the table, talking to Snider as he selected the goldpieces from the mixture he held. "I'll keep that promise, of course, whenever I need a man in this part of the country," he said casually. "But I hired you only to bring in the woman, this time. You've done well, so I'm giving you fifty dollars more than I agreed to pay for the job. When I need you again, I'll find you."

"That ain't the deal we made!" Snider said hotly.

Rader's voice was as icy as Snider's had been heated. "Take your money and go, Snider."

"Like hell I will! You think I'm gonna leave you to have your fun with the Starbuck woman before I get a whack at her?"

"Nothing was said about that," Rader told him.

"I don't give a shit what was said and what wasn't! I never have had a chance to put it into a fancy piece like her, and I don't aim to pass up this one! You can have her first, if you want, but I get my turn when you're done!"

Rader opened his mouth to reply to Snider's angry ultimatum, but before he could say anything, Jessie saw the ugly frown on his face change into an equally ugly smile.

"Maybe I spoke too soon," he told Snider. "The Starbuck woman doesn't appeal to me, but it might be useful to give her a taste of what's waiting for her. Go ahead, Snider. She's yours for the rest of the night. Do whatever you want with her."

After he'd ridden for a mile or so down the center of the wide, hoof-pocked trail left by the herd, Ki's keen sense of logic gradually overcame his anger and concern. He began trying to recall features of the land over which they'd driven the herd from Palo Duro Creek to the North Fork of the Canadian. Thinking of the river, he realized that its location, north of the wide trail he was following, would form a natural barrier to anyone traveling that way.

Ki reined his pony to the south edge of the broken ground and continued to follow it, riding at its edge. He'd covered another mile and was beginning to doubt the reasoning that a short time ago had seemed so valid, when he saw a soft gleam on the ground, a dot shining in the moonlight.

Riding up to the source of the gleam, Ki reined in the horse and dismounted. When he picked up the silver dollar, his mind went at once to Tascosa and the Howard & McMasters Store, where Jessie had not only obtained a large number of silver dollars, but where they'd first encountered Snider.

"Good for you, Jessie," Ki muttered as he swung back into the saddle. "You've given me a trail to follow. Now all I must do is reach the end of it in time!"

For a moment Snider stared at Rader, confused by the cartel operative's sudden change of mind. He asked, "You mean that?"

"If I hadn't meant it, I wouldn't have said it," Rader replied. "Go ahead. A little of your rough treatment now might make her more willing to cooperate when we question her later."

As she'd listened to Rader and Snider arguing, Jessie had felt a cold knot of anger forming in her stomach. Surrendering to a man of her own free will was one thing, but this was quite another. She'd been threatened before with rape, but had always managed to escape before the threat could be carried out. This rape, she told herself, might be the one she couldn't escape.

She looked at Snider, who was still staring at Rader as though he couldn't believe what the man had just said. Jessie turned her eyes toward Rader. After delivering her into the hands of Snider, he'd walked to the chair that stood a few feet from the table and settled into it. He was watching Jessie and Snider now, his face as expressionless as a mask, his eyes cold and implacable.

A grin of anticipation formed on Snider's face. He stepped

over to the chair where Jessie sat, and looked down at her as he started unbuckling his gunbelt. "I been wanting to put the prong to you ever since the first time I saw you," he said gloatingly. "I don't guess I'll be the first one, but I bet I'll be the one you remember the longest."

Hanging his gunbelt on the back of the chair, Snider lifted Jessie's feet and pulled her boots off. In his eagerness, he did not notice the weight of the derringer in her right boot, and the safety strap on the holster of the wicked little gun kept it from falling when he tossed the boot aside. Pulling Jessie roughly to her feet, he took off her gunbelt and was about to rip open the fly of her jeans when Rader spoke.

"You fool, don't tear her clothes!" he said. "I'll be taking her through towns where people might ask questions if anything's wrong with her clothing!"

"Damn it, Rader, I wanta get at this pretty bitch!" Snider replied. He unbuttoned his jeans and pulled them below his hips, letting his engorged member spring free. "Look at that! I got a hard-on here that won't quit!"

"Don't display yourself to me," Rader told him coldly. "If you're in such a hurry, get busy with the woman."

Snider turned back to Jessie. After her first glimpse of his erection, she had kept her eyes fixed on the cabin wall, her head high, her jaws clamped tightly shut.

"You ever had one like mine before?" he asked as his fingers worked eagerly at the buttons of her jeans. When Jessie did not reply, Snider went on, "Go on, make out like you're too good for me! You won't act so high and mighty when you feel me jam this into you!"

Lifting Jessie bodily, Snider carried her to the table. He laid her on it and yanked off her jeans, looked at her knee-length pantalettes, and ripped them off without taking time to find their buttons. Jessie lay staring at the ceiling, using all her willpower to make her mind blank and to hold herself firmly in control, but she tensed involuntarily when Snider grabbed her knees and forced her thighs apart.

With a crash, the door of the cabin burst open and Ki leaped through it. His jump carried him well into the room. He had a *shuriken* in each hand.

Rader leaped from his chair and started toward Ki, his hand clawing for his pistol grips. Ki paid no attention to the cartel operative; his eyes were on Snider.

Ki launched one of the *shuriken*. The shining, star-shaped blade spun through the air and sank into Snider's throat. Blood bubbled around the edges of the *shuriken* imbedded in his neck as Snider's knees buckled and he began collapsing, his mouth still open in a surprised gape.

Jessie had opened her eyes when the door burst open. Rader had his gun out when she turned to look at him, and was leveling the revolver at Ki. Jessie kicked his extended hand. The pistol sailed out of his grasp and dropped near the cabin wall.

Ki saw Rader going to retrieve his revolver, and covered the distance between them with a single great leap. He landed just behind Rader and swept his bent arm around in a powerful *ushiro-hiji* strike. The point of Ki's elbow hit Rader's spine at the base of his skull. There was a loud pop as his neck snapped. His spinal cord severed, Rader slumped lifeless to the floor.

Jessie was sitting on the edge of the table when Ki turned away from Rader's body. She'd pulled her blouse down as far as possible, but her bare thighs and legs were shining in the light of the lantern.

She raised her forearms as high as she could with the rope still binding her elbows, and tugged at the noose around her neck. Drawing his *tanto* as he stepped to the table, Ki sliced through the ropes with the keen-edged blade, and they fell away.

"I'm getting chilled without my jeans, Ki," Jessie said. "If you wouldn't mind handing them to me..."

Ki picked the jeans up from the floor and handed them to her, then busied himself dragging Snider's corpse away from the table while Jessie pulled on the jeans.

"I hated to put you through what just happened," he apologized as Jessie slid off the table and fastened the top button of her denims. "But if I'd broken in before they moved close together, where I was sure I could handle them without your being harmed, my surprise attack might not have succeeded."

Jessie had gone to the chair where her boots lay, and was pulling them on. She looked up and asked, "You mean you were watching all the time?"

Ki nodded. "Through a crack in the door. It was the light shining through it that led me here, after I'd followed the trail you left."

Jessie finished pulling on her boots and stood up. She said, "I suppose you saw—"

Ki broke in, "I saw only what I needed to see to get you free."

"Yes, of course," Jessie said thoughtfully. She looked around the room, then gestured toward the two bodies. "What shall we do with them, Ki?"

"Leave them. In this wild country, bodies are found and buried without causing too much excitement."

"I suppose so," Jessie agreed. "Besides, we have a herd of cattle waiting at the river. And even though the devil himself seems to have been dogging our trail all the way from the Circle Star, we're going to deliver those steers to market at Dodge City, and then we'll take the first train home, where we can relax!"